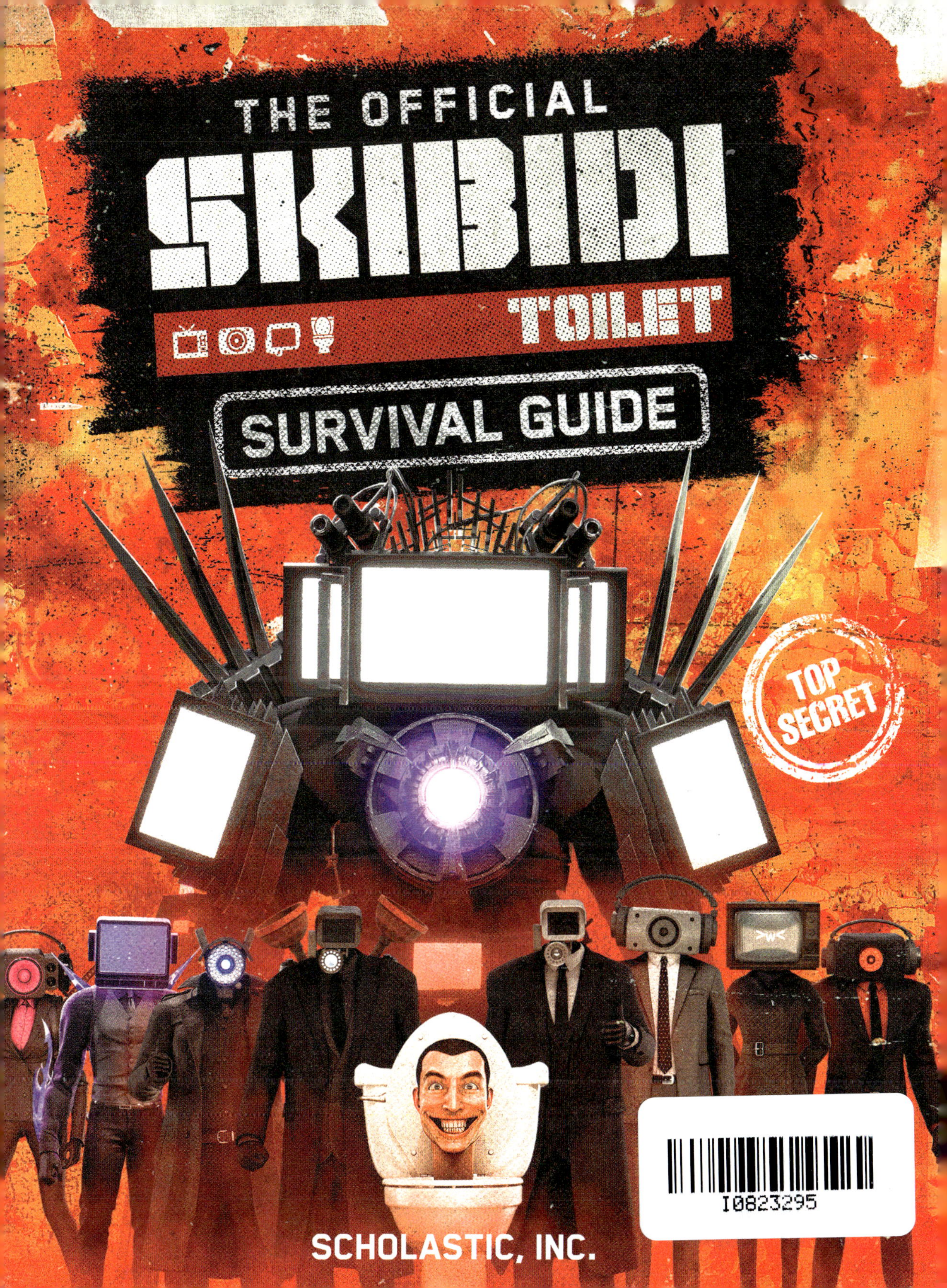
THE OFFICIAL
SKIBIDI
TOILET
SURVIVAL GUIDE
TOP SECRET
SCHOLASTIC, INC.

ISBN: 979-8-2250-1232-8

10 9 8 7 6 5 4 3 2 1 25 26 27 28 29

Printed in the U.S.A. 40

First printing 2025

Book design by Martha Maynard

THE OFFICIAL SKIBIDI TOILET SURVIVAL GUIDE

HOW TO USE THESE NOTES

This is an attempt to bring together all the information about the war, the different factions fighting it, and the main players. The situation keeps changing, so this is a snapshot of the situation as best I can tell right now. Feel free to add your own notes as more is discovered. I WILL.

Recordings of the conflict have helped formulate these notes, but they are incomplete. Where information comes from specific files, these files are referenced with the sources. Everything is as accurate as possible, and pictures have been included where they exist.

I hope these help you survive. Good luck.

PLUNGERMAN

SKIBIDI TOILETS

They came from the stars to conquer Earth. And they came singing . . .

The Skibidi Toilets have heads that look human, sticking out of a toilet that can move. When they first came, people thought they were harmless. Maybe weird, but harmless. But they came to kill all humans and take over Earth. If you hear their anthem . . . well, it may already be too late for you.

Nobody knows much about how they operate, or why they chose this form, but we've scraped together everything we do know.

DAILY NEWS

BUSINESS • POLITICS • ECONOMICS • ENTERTAINMENT • SPORTS • WEATHER

BREAKING NEWS

HEADS SEEN IN TOILETS

PLUMBERS BAFFLED!

After receiving a series of reports that singing heads have been appearing inside toilets across the city, police have been forced to accept these are not prank calls. More worryingly, some people who have encountered these heads have since disappeared.

Police have no leads on who might be responsible, but have reassured the public that no one can enter their home through their toilet.

"It's just not possible for a man to crawl up out of a toilet," an official statement said. "An octopus could do it, sure. But a person? Nah."

SKIBIDI TOILETS

	SPECIES **SKIBIDI TOILET**
	OCCUPATION **FOOT SOLDIER**
	FACTION **TOILET**
	HEIGHT **3 FEET 11 INCHES**

CRITICAL INFORMATION

There used to be a lot of base model Toilets, but they are not around so much anymore. They always got treated as expendable, and didn't seem to mind sacrificing themselves. It's likely that they all either got killed or upgraded into something else. I BELIEVE THEY'RE EXTINCT AT THIS POINT.

They also were used for experiments a lot . . . Base model Toilets aren't particularly designed for battle, and they usually attack by ramming, biting, and headbutting their opponents. But, don't take them lightly if you see one.

Sometimes the Toilets seem to be mocking humanity by doing human-type things. There have been reports of Cop Toilets with flashing lights on their cisterns and even a Saint Toilet with a halo in a church . . .

The white-base model Toilets mostly seem to have been replaced by the gray versions. These are like Skibidi Toilets 2.0—they're more aggressive and tougher to kill. White is easier to see on the battlefield than gray, so the white models were easier targets.

INTELLECTUAL THEFT

Lots of the gray Normal Toilets wear protective sunglasses to avoid the TV Men's attacks. These glasses were created by their Chief Scientist after they managed to get hold of a Cameraman's lens.

IT'S CRITICAL THAT WE PROTECT OUR TECHNOLOGY AT ALL COST!

ORIGINAL BASE MODEL TOILETS DIDN'T HAVE THE JETPACKS PICTURED HERE—IT WAS JUST LATER WAVES OF TOILETS THAT WERE EQUIPPED FOR FLIGHT (FILE 39). I WONDER WHO THEY STOLE THIS TECH FROM!

-CAMERAWOMAN

PARASITE SKIBIDI TOILET

	SPECIES **SKIBIDI TOILET**
	OCCUPATION **FOOT SOLDIER**
	FACTION **TOILET**
	HEIGHT **15.75 INCHES** DON'T UNDERESTIMATE THEM.

CRITICAL INFORMATION

These four-legged Toilets are small but deadly. They cling onto a host's body and use an extendable metal tongue to inject them with a parasite. The parasite then takes over the mind of the host and makes them turn on their comrades (file 30).

The Toilets infected several Speakermen and Cameramen this way, and even managed to get Titan Speakerman using two larger Parasites (file 32).

Fortunately the Chief Scientist Cameraman developed the Parasite Disabler Gun. With this you can shoot the host and kill the parasite inside (file 35). Unfortunately it wasn't effective on Titan Speakerman . . .

WORKED EVENTUALLY, THOUGH. THE SKIBIDI TOILETS HAD TO TURN TO OTHER WEAPONS AFTER WE DEVELOPED THIS DEFENSE.

THE ORIGINAL PARASITES SEEM TO HAVE DIED OUT— BUT WE SOMETIMES SEE THE LARGER VARIANTS.

GLITCH SKIBIDI TOILET

	SPECIES **SKIBIDI TOILET**
	OCCUPATION **FOOT SOLDIER**
	FACTION **TOILET**
	HEIGHT **6 FEET 5 INCHES**

CRITICAL INFORMATION

Research suggests that this was another of the Chief Scientist's creations. He had a dark normal base, but could be identified by the control panel behind his head. He didn't seem to have a handle, but even if he did, you couldn't reach it to flush him anyway—because he had the ability to perform a sonic charge. This meant he could move faster than the speed of sound. He also had three armor plates mounted on the front of his toilet, making his charge attacks even more brutally effective.

Finally, the Alliance encountered him again. TV Woman hypnotized him, then Scientist Cameraman neutralized him (file 54), and they took him to the lab.

WE'RE LUCKY THEY DIDN'T DEVELOP MORE GLITCH TOILETS—I DON'T KNOW WHY THEY DIDN'T. MAYBE THEY COULDN'T, OR MAYBE THEY HAD PROBLEMS WITH THE TECH, OR MAYBE HE WAS HARD TO CONTROL?

DJ SKIBIDI TOILET

	SPECIES **SKIBIDI TOILET**
	OCCUPATION **FOOT SOLDIER**
	FACTION **TOILET**
	HEIGHT **65 FEET**

CRITICAL INFORMATION

It's easy to identify the DJ from his gray beanie and headphones. He sings his own remix version of the Anthem, too, and can levitate. He was first seen in a nightclub in Ohio, playing music to Toilets and humans, but when a Cameraman approached him, he attacked (file 6). No sightings of him were reported for a long time, and he was thought dead.

WE SHOULD BE SO LUCKY.

The DJ Toilet later came back with a big upgrade. The Mech version of the DJ still wore his beanie and headphones, but he also had sunglasses and Strider legs (file 70).

His Pioneer DJ turntable is attached to his body, and for maximum sonic power he has banks of speakers mounted on the back and front of his toilet. He also has four laser cannons and an auxiliary cannon.

OVERKILL, BUT THIS WAS NOTHING COMPARED TO WHAT WAS TO COME . . .

VERSION 2.0

THE SECOND VERSION OF THE DJ TOILET WAS THOUGHT TO BE DESTROYED BY THE DETAINER ASTRO TOILET, BUT HE RETURNED WITH ANOTHER NEW FORM, INCLUDING NEW SPEAKERS, A JETPACK, AND A HOODIE (FILE 77).

BUZZSAW SKIBIDI TOILET

	SPECIES **SKIBIDI TOILET**
	OCCUPATION **AERIAL ATTACK**
	FACTION **TOILET**
	HEIGHT **9 FEET**

CRITICAL INFORMATION

Another variant created by the Toilets' Chief Scientist, based on a gray Toilet. Not the biggest, but utterly deadly thanks to his flying ability and the large buzzsaw fitted to his base. He also wore goggles that protected him against the TV Men's light attacks, and had twin guns attached to his cistern.

I FOUGHT THE BUZZSAW TOILET MYSELF IN NEW YORK CITY—HE MANAGED TO CUT A CAMERAMAN IN HALF.

MULTIFORMS

Several variants of the Buzzsaw have been seen on the battlefield, including a Strider, a Quad-Buzzsaw version, and a Mutant. The Dual Buzzsaw Car (file 61)—a wheeled Toilet with side-mounted blades—seemed formidable at first, but a paralyzing laser blast caused him to veer off the road and crash into a truck.

THE BUZZSAW TOILET I ENCOUNTERED LATER TOOK DOWN SEVERAL CAMERAMEN AND DECAPITATED A SPEAKERMAN (FILE 48). BRUTAL. BUT TV WOMAN TURNED THAT BATTLE AROUND. SHE TOOK OVER HIS MIND AND TURNED HIM AGAINST THE OTHER TOILETS, DESTROYING A FLYING ARTILLERY TOILET—AND CAUSING AN EXPLOSION THAT TOOK THE BUZZSAW TOILET WITH IT (FILE 49).

CHIEF SCIENTIST SKIBIDI TOILET

	SPECIES **SKIBIDI TOILET**
	OCCUPATION **CHIEF SCIENTIST**
	FACTION **TOILET**
	HEIGHT **14–19 FEET**

CRITICAL INFORMATION

Arguably the most important member of the Toilet faction. He only answers to G-Toilet, and he creates most of their technology. Upgrades, variants, weapons—most of it comes directly from him, including upgrades to G-Toilet himself. You can identify him from his head, which looks older than most Toilets' heads. Apart from that, his original form isn't really any different from any other Toilet's.

The Chief Scientist is not to be confused with the Grandfather Skibidi Toilet, the other white-haired Toilet we've encountered (file 14).

The Alliance sent in their own Camera Toilet to infiltrate his laboratory, where they saw him working with his team of scientists (file 16). That was where they created the first Striders. There was an explosion—but the Chief Scientist survived . . .

THE GRANDFATHER DOESN'T WEAR GLASSES.

OF COURSE HE DID . . .

SCIENTIFIC UPGRADES

The Chief Scientist resurfaced in his larger, Version 2.0 body (file 30). This featured a metal toilet with claws mounted on the sides, a long robotic arm, and a disgusting new ability to produce small Parasite Toilets from his mouth.

WE HAVE FOOTAGE OF THIS IF YOU REALLY WANT TO SEE THE PROCESS IN ACTION. I DON'T RECOMMEND WATCHING IT.

PARASITES

WATCH FOR THE SIGNS

Keep an eye on your fellow Cameramen and Speakermen.

1. Do they have a Parasite Toilet attached to them—especially their neck?
2. Are they screaming?
3. Are there blue sparks around their head?
4. Are their fingers becoming stretched?
5. Is their head constantly shaking?
6. Are they singing the Skibidi Anthem?

If the answer to any of these questions is "yes," use the Disabler Gun IMMEDIATELY.

GETTING INVOLVED

We didn't see the Chief Scientist again for a long time, and when we did he'd upgraded again, taking on an even larger Mech form (file 67). He used to work behind the scenes, rather than fighting on the front lines—but not anymore. Now, as well as his Strider legs and jetpack, he has a laser cannon.

OBSERVATIONS

Maybe the Chief Scientist figured out we'd target him. Last time I ran into him, I took a hit from one of those laser blasts. He's taken charge of Alpha-Hills Labs for his experiments. We're planning a raid soon. We should've taken him out a long time ago. Without him the Toilets will be that much weaker.

—Plungerman

... Skibidi Toilet.

PLUNGERMAN DIDN'T SURVIVE THAT RAID (FILE 70). THIS WAS ONE OF THE LAST THINGS HE WROTE.

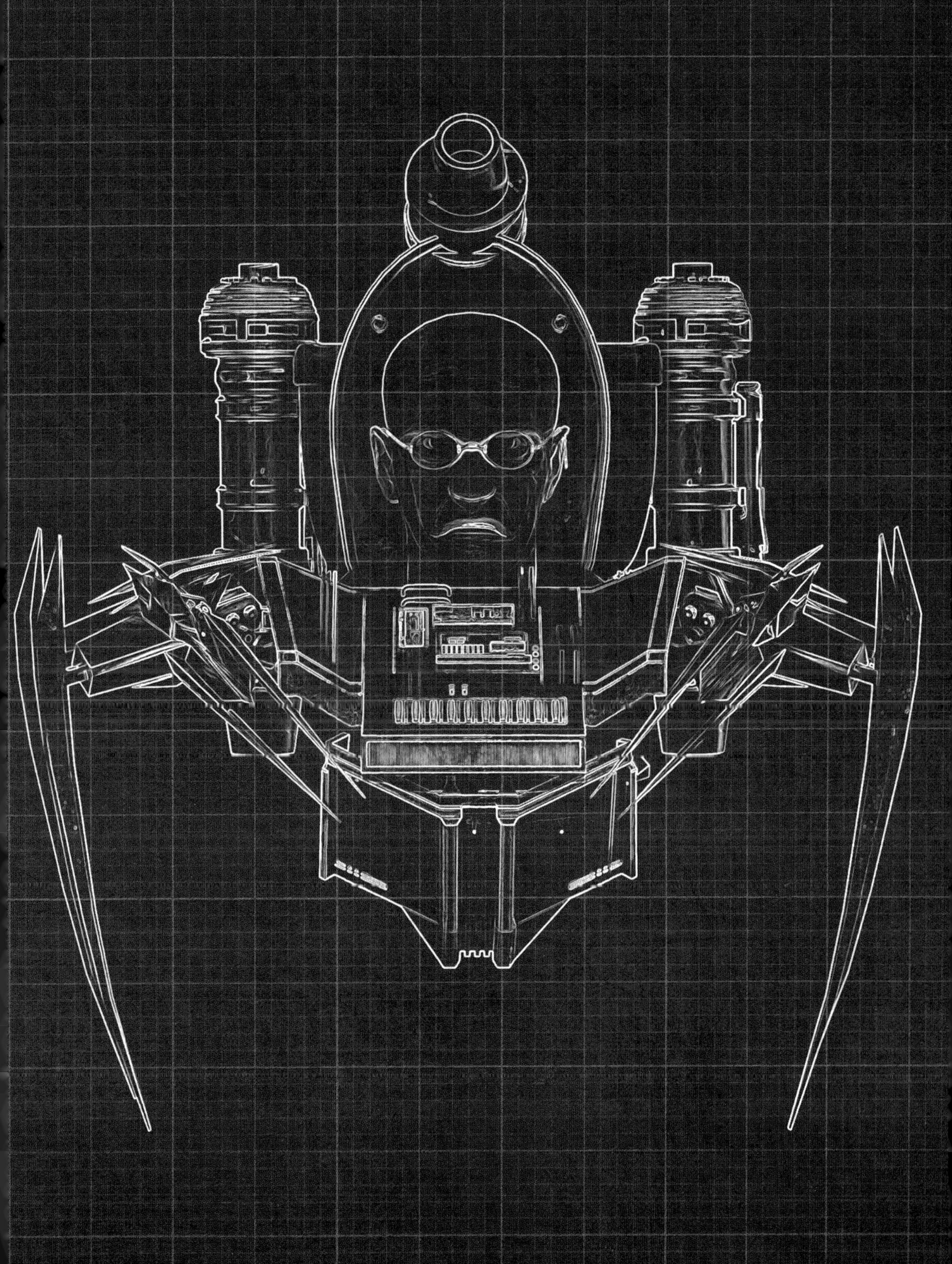

G-TOILET

	SPECIES **SKIBIDI TOILET**
	OCCUPATION **COMMANDER**
	FACTION **TOILET**
	HEIGHT **UNKNOWN**

CRITICAL INFORMATION

SERIOUS BEFORE . . .

The war started to get serious when G-Toilet appeared on the scene (file 7)—although it seems likely he was on Earth from the start, but just didn't show his face until the other Toilets began to invade. Some think he created the Toilets on Earth, but for now that's just a theory.

RIGHT NOW WE NEED FACTS, THOUGH.

In his original form, G-Toilet was much like any other Toilet, but larger and with the ability to shoot lasers from his eyes. This ability seems to be genetic, rather than coming from any extra technology. Only he and the Giant Flying Skibidi Toilet can do this (file 13). He will also fight at close quarters, using headbutts, biting, ramming, or whatever else works at the time. And he's unflushable.

SOMETHING TO BE GRATEFUL FOR, I SUPPOSE.

G-FORCE

G-Toilet has undergone several upgrades since the start of the war—perhaps he was surprised by the level of resistance he encountered, and the Alliance sending out its own Titans (file 35).

DON'T BE FOOLED!

G-MAN TOILET HAS BEEN KNOWN TO USE DECOYS THAT LOOK EXACTLY LIKE HIM, AND ARE JUST AS STRONG. YOU MAY THINK YOU'VE BEATEN HIM, BUT HE COULD STILL BE OUT THERE!

He added two side-mounted laser cannons and a jetpack, as well as changing his color to gray. He then increased his size and upped his laser cannons to six, as well as adopting headphones and yellow sunglasses for protection (file 57).

REACTION TIME

After a further increase in size, he changed his color to black and took up wearing black sunglasses, replaced his six laser cannons with two large ones, and added a reactor core (file 67). After coming close to destruction at the hands of the three Alliance Titans (file 74), then joining forces with the Alliance against the Astro Toilets, he came back with yet another new design, including face-mounted laser cannons and mechanical claws (file 77).

Other Toilets will often put themselves in unnecessary danger, and seem willing to sacrifice themselves for the Toilet cause. G-Toilet isn't like that. He's always got troops around him, and if he feels like a battle is turning against him, he'll retreat and come back to fight another day.

THE EXACT NATURE OF G-TOILET'S RELATIONSHIP TO THE ASTRO TOILETS IS UNCLEAR. COULD HE HAVE BEEN A COMMANDER IN THE ASTRO FACTION? WHAT IS THE ORIGIN OF HIS ISSUES WITH THE ASSAILANT ASTRO TOILET?

SWAT MUTANT

	SPECIES **SKIBIDI MUTANT**
	OCCUPATION **G-SQUAD MEMBER**
	FACTION **UNKNOWN**
	HEIGHT **UNKNOWN**–LARGE

DOES HE HAVE SOME CONNECTION TO THE POLICE TOILETS?*

CRITICAL INFORMATION

As his name suggests, this Mutant wears SWAT gear on his humanoid body (file 72). He carries the kind of gear you'd expect a human SWAT officer to use—a riot shield, a riot helmet, a machine gun, rocket launchers, a sickle . . . actually maybe he goes a little further than the typical SWAT officer. He's been seen on the battlefield with SWAT Toilets wielding axes, but those all seem to have been wiped out.

After a round of upgrades, he came back with two cyber-sickles, energy-based weapons that he can throw with great accuracy (file 77). With these he can decapitate multiple targets at once. He's the only Toilet to use sickles, and it's his most distinctive weapon. Even though he's equipped with three machine guns now, he never seems to use them. He's now become a member of G-Squad.

* WE USED TO SEE THEM DURING THE EARLY DAYS OF THE WAR (FILE 9). THEY WORE POLICE HATS AND HAD SIRENS ON TOP OF THEIR CISTERNS. WE THOUGHT WE'D SEEN THE LAST OF THOSE, BUT THEN A HEAVILY ARMED SPEARGUN VARIANT TURNED UP (FILE 65) AND WAS LATER FOUND GUARDING THE ENTRANCE TO ALPHA-HILLS (FILE 67).

BUZZSAW MUTANT

	SPECIES **SKIBIDI MUTANT**
	OCCUPATION **G-SQUAD MEMBER**
	FACTION **UNKNOWN**
	HEIGHT **UNKNOWN**–LARGE

CRITICAL INFORMATION

Like other Mutants, the Buzzsaw Mutant has a humanoid body seemingly harvested from a felled member of the Alliance—in his case, the body of a Large Cameraman. His most notable feature is that his right hand has been replaced by a buzzsaw (file 62). In his upgraded form, the Buzzsaw Mutant also has a laser cannon fitted to his right arm, and is equipped with cyber katanas (file 71). The cyber katanas have energy blades and can be recalled to his hand after being thrown or dropped.

CALM IN A CRISIS

The Buzzsaw Mutant approaches combat in a casual manner, taking his time over kills. He has often fought alongside the Berserker Mutant, allowing the Berserker to distract opponents while he springs an ambush (file 62).

HE HAS ONLY ONE HAND, BUT CARRIES TWO KATANAS. I GUESS THE OTHER IS A SPARE IN CASE ONE GETS BROKEN?

He successfully resisted an attack by Large TV Man, putting on sunglasses quickly enough to protect himself (file 66). After joining G-Squad, the Buzzsaw Mutant was one of those who took on a Specialist Astro Toilet (file 77): It was his cyber katana that saved the life of a Cameraman at the start of the union between the Skibidi Toilets and the Alliance.

FEMALE MUTANT

	SPECIES **SKIBIDI MUTANT**
	OCCUPATION **ELITE FIGHTER**
	FACTION **UNKNOWN**
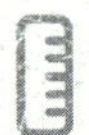	HEIGHT **UNKNOWN**–MEDIUM

CRITICAL INFORMATION

A small number of female Skibidi Toilets were seen during the early days of the war (e.g., file 14), but they seemed to vanish from the ranks entirely—until the Female Skibidi Mutant rocked up to pitch in with the battle against the Astro Toilets (file 75). In her initial form, she was armed with a laser cannon on her left arm and four clawed blades mounted on her back. She delivered the final blow to the Scout Astro Toilet that had threatened to overwhelm a group of Cameramen and Skibidi Toilets.

UNLIKELY SAVIORS

As the new Alliance began to make use of salvaged Astro technology, the Female Mutant was upgraded and equipped with shoulder-mounted Astro Destruction Lasers (file 77). She made the point that a number of Alliance fighters had been abandoned by their own side, and it was left to the Skibidi faction to rescue them.

As best we can tell, the Female Mutant used to be a police officer. She had been searching for her sister, a national guard, at Alpha-Hills (File 73). She had a photograph of her sister, who we recognized as the Female Mutant before her modification at the hands of the Toilets.

BERSERKER MUTANT

	SPECIES **SKIBIDI MUTANT**
	OCCUPATION **G-SQUAD LEADER**
	FACTION **MUTANT**
	HEIGHT **36 FEET**

CRITICAL INFORMATION

The Berserker was one of the first Mutant Toilets encountered, along with the Buzzsaw Mutant. The Mutants have Toilet heads but humanoid bodies. It is suspected the bodies come from dead Alliance fighters.

The Berserker has the body of a Large Speakerman. He's strong—he tore a Cameraman clean in half—and he uses a jetpack. He seems to have his face pinned into a permanent grin. NOT THE HAPPY KIND.

He was believed to be killed after being hit with a barrage from the air, which injured and blinded him. He lost his headphones in the attack, so a Large Speakerman hit him with a sound wave and then stabbed him in the head.

He came back with a new, upgraded form. Mutants are tougher than regular Toilets. The Berserker 2.0 doesn't wear a shirt like his previous version. He wears sunglasses and a bandanna. PROBABLY TO COVER UP THE SCAR WHERE HE GOT STABBED.

In addition to his jetpack, he's got laser cannons and a hook attached to each arm.

NEW ALLIANCES

When the Berserker showed up again, he'd joined G-Squad. He killed one Cameraman with his lasers, crushed another, and was only stopped from killing a Camerawoman because the Scientist Mech showed up.

Once he joined forces with the Alliance, the Berserker became a huge asset on the field of battle. In one skirmish he took out several Astro Toilets, crushing the head of one, ripping the head off another and using it as a weapon to destroy another, and pulling an Interceptor out of the sky (file 77).

AND FAILED.

Having tried to destroy Camerawoman last time they met, he seemed appreciative of her upgrades when fighting alongside her. He's undergone further upgrades himself, using Astro technology to improve his laser cannons, as well as strengthening his armor.

> "Relax. We ain't here to hurt nobody. Time for us to become friends . . . Officially ;)"
>
> BERSERKER MUTANT

THEN THE ASTRO TOILETS ARRIVED, AND EVERYTHING CHANGED. BERSERKER AND BUZZSAW SHOWED UP AGAIN DURING A FIGHT WITH ASTRO TOILETS AND SAVED THE LIFE OF A CAMERAMAN. THEY WANTED TO JOIN FORCES.

THE CAMERAMAN TRIED TO REJECT THE OFFER. HE DIDN'T TRUST IT. UNDERSTANDABLY. BUT YOU DON'T GET THAT OPTION WHERE THE MUTANTS ARE CONCERNED. THEY JUST DO THEIR PEAK ALPHA MALE LAUGH, AND THERE'S NO DISAGREEING WITH THAT.

SO THE BERSERKER ENDED UP BEING AN IMPORTANT PART OF BRINGING THE ALLIANCE TOGETHER WITH THE SKIBIDI TOILETS. I DON'T THINK ANYONE PREDICTED THAT.

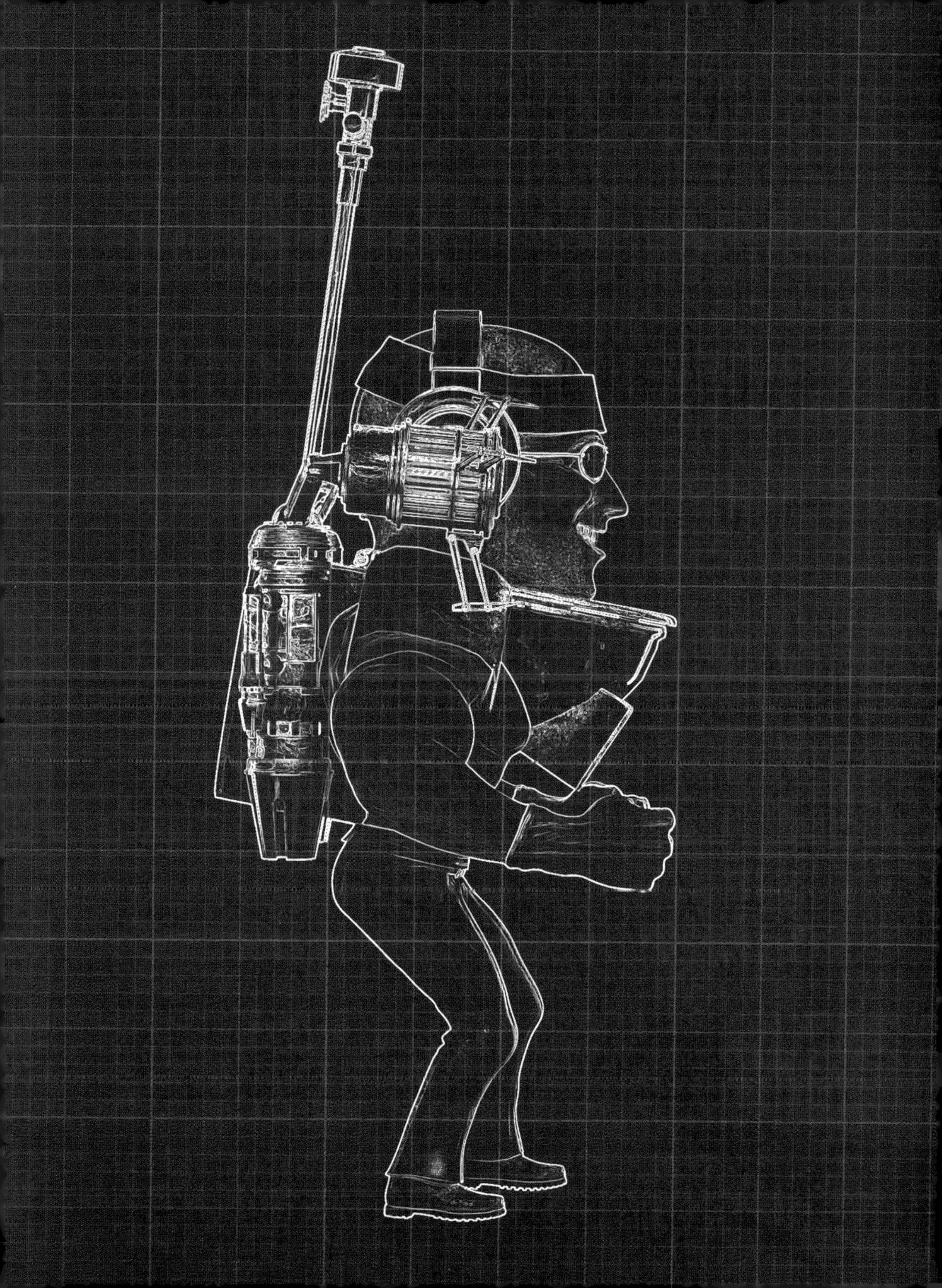

ATTACK STRATEGIES

The Toilets have a basic weakness: You can flush the head using the handle at the top of the cistern. However, this involves getting close to the Toilet, and if you approach from the front, you have to reach past the head.

ATTACK IN PAIRS

One person can attack an isolated Toilet from the front while the other approaches from the back and flushes them.

TARGET THE HEAD

A quick punch to the uncovered head of a Toilet doesn't have to do serious damage—if it stuns them for a moment, that could be your chance to hit the flush.

PLUNGER FORCE

While plungers need to be applied at close range, they have proven to be highly effective.

RETREAT TACTICS

Don't take on Toilets larger than yourself! Leave those to fighters of equal size. Don't pick fights you can't win!

THE ALLIANCE

The Skibidi Toilets seemed to have taken over the world, with few—~~if any~~—human survivors. Their victory seemed inevitable . . . but then the resistance emerged. These heroes are a group of humanoids with audiovisual equipment for heads, known only as the Alliance.

THE ALLIANCE NEEDS YOU

Help us free the world from the Toilet menace! As well as frontline fighters, the Alliance needs skills such as:

>>>Espionage
>>>Repair
>>>Research
>>>Tech development
>>>Engineering
>>>Medics

JOIN TODAY

THE CAMERAMEN

	SPECIES	CAMERAMAN
	OCCUPATION	FOOT SOLDIER
	FACTION	CAMERA
	HEIGHT	6 FEET 6 INCHES

CRITICAL INFORMATION

AND WOMEN!

Cameramen are the backbone of the Alliance. With cameras for heads, they record footage of everything they see. This is why the Camera faction has so much data on the conflict. Even if a Cameraman falls in battle, the Alliance can get hold of their footage and learn from it.

Below the neck, they wear suits and ties—and all they need to communicate is a thumbs-up (or, if necessary, a thumbs-down).

A PROPER OUTFIT IS IMPORTANT FOR MORALE.

Most Cameramen are equipped with a CCTV-style camera, but some have movie cameras or camcorders. As the war went on, headphones became standard equipment, to protect from sonic weapons (file 25).

PLUS YOU GET REALLY SICK HEARING THAT ANTHEM WHEN YOU'RE OUT ON THE BATTLEFIELD.

In the early days of the war, the Toilets had the upper hand on us. But we've developed our technology and weaponry, as well as our strategy.

ALSO, WE'RE SIMPLY BETTER. WE JUST ARE.

PLUNGERMAN

	SPECIES **CAMERAMAN**
	OCCUPATION **INFILTRATOR**
	FACTION  **CAMERA**
	HEIGHT **6 FEET 7 INCHES**

CRITICAL INFORMATION

This member of the Black Cameramen faction has become a major figure in the conflict, and is known as Plungerman due to his use of plungers as close-combat weapons (file 43). Earlier in the war he wore a red tie, but later changed this to black.

Plungerman is also equipped with retractable claws in his fists, which he can use to inflict extra damage, and upgrades have added a jetpack to his equipment. He also drives the Glitchmobile, which has become his main offensive weapon other than plungers.

Plungerman doesn't appear in much footage taken during the early part of the war, but he's always been with the Alliance since the start. Some have speculated he was once a human known as Dave.

DANGEROUS OPERATIVE

While Plungerman has a reputation for bravery, some Alliance members say he's also reckless.

The TV Men often say Cameramen take too many foolish risks, and when they say this, really they're talking about Plungerman. He's taken a number of injuries during the course of the war, including the loss of a leg while fighting the Fast Armored Toilet. He was also badly crushed when the Alliance tried to release the Titan Speakerman from infection (file 57).

Although he is not the only Alliance member to use plungers against the Toilets, his fighting style is memorable (file 55).

Advantages of plungers:

- Light.
- Easy to carry.
- Easy to use.
- Simple to manufacture.
- Don't need a power source.
- Don't need software updates.

They are excellent weapons. Hard to improve upon, but the spiked versions definitely add something (file 69). He will use guns if necessary, but he finds a plunger kill more satisfying.

Listen, sometimes you have to take the chance to strike, or it'll slip away from you. I'm not one to watch opportunities slide down the toilet. And hey, I've survived more battles than almost any other Cameraman out there. Maybe I'm just lucky, who knows?

IF NOT FOR HIM, SO MANY OF OUR ALLIES WOULD NOT BE HERE TODAY. IF NOT FOR HIM, WE MAY NOT HAVE EVEN HAD A WORLD TO FIGHT FOR ANYMORE.

Plungerman was killed during the Siege of Alpha-Hills (File 70). If not for him, we might not have survived long enough to unite with the Skibidi Toilets against the Astro Toilets. He remains an inspiration to us all.

CAMERAWOMAN

	SPECIES **CAMERAMAN**
	OCCUPATION **FIELD COMMANDER**
	FACTION **CAMERA**
	HEIGHT **6 FEET**

CRITICAL INFORMATION

Identifiable from her black trench coat and the cyan light from her cylinder camera (a very different design than that of most Cameramen), Camerawoman is a major figure in the Alliance and one of only a small number of female Alliance fighters. She has worked directly alongside her counterparts, TV Woman and Speakerwoman (file 66).

In her earlier form she made use of a bolt rifle fitted to her back, giving her a turret mounted above her head that could be used for ranged attacks: When finding targets, her camera light would turn red (file 52). One of her earliest contributions to the war effort was to help tackle the G-Toilet during the fight to disinfect Titan Speakerman (file 57).

SECRET ORIGINS

No comment.

There's a theory that Camerawoman was once a human called Cathy, and that her friend and colleague Dave was the human form of Plungerman, who Camerawoman worked with many times during the war.

MODERN ARSENAL

Camerawoman's weaponry was later revised. Instead of the bolt rifle fitted above her head, she was given a bolt rifle on each arm and the space above her head was taken by a laser rifle (file 70). She took a major injury during the Siege of Alpha-Hills, losing an arm in an explosion created by the Acid Striker Skibidi Toilet (file 73).

NEW TOOLS

After the death of Plungerman, Camerawoman started using his signature spiked plunger, taking out multiple Toilets with it (file 73), and since then has often been referred to as Plungerwoman. She took on a new appearance, discarding her black trench coat in favor of a black jumpsuit and military beret (file 77).

THE JUMPSUIT LACKS THE SWISH OF THE OLD TRENCH COAT, BUT IT'S MORE PRACTICAL.

CRITICAL ROLE

Camerawoman also has all-new weaponry in this upgrade, including shoulder-mounted lasers and two gravitational plungers. Since the death of Plungerman, she has become a major focal point for the Alliance.

I WANT IT ON THE RECORD THAT I PROTESTED THE TV MEN ALLOWING ALLIANCE FIGHTERS TO DIE SO THEY COULD SALVAGE ASTRO TECH.

THAT'S NOT HOW WE DO THINGS.

LARGE CAMERAMEN

	SPECIES **CAMERAMAN**
	OCCUPATION **SUPPORT UNITS**
	FACTION **CAMERA**
	HEIGHT **19 FEET**

CRITICAL INFORMATION

The Large Cameramen have been an important part of the Alliance forces since the beginning of the war (file 3). Due to the Skibidi Toilets fielding many large combat units, the Alliance needed troops able to counter this. Large Cameramen are not just larger versions of Normal Cameramen: Their heads take the form of movie cameras, rather than the CCTV cameras of the Normals.

Large Cameramen have been equipped with paralyzer laser rifles and rocket launchers. They can bear much heavier weapons than Normal Cameramen, and this is their main function on the battlefield. As well as being larger, they're stronger and more durable, and can take out several Normal Toilets without any issues (files 12 and 18). Later versions of the Large Cameramen have been fitted with jetpacks to counter their slow movement, as well as dual rocket launchers (file 66), and they have also used chainswords (file 77).

The Large Cameramen's camera heads are adapted to carry electronic signals. If they were old-style movie cameras, it would complicate matters—their POV would only be accessible by developing the film from their heads—and fighters wouldn't be able to tap into them live during combat.

NOT TO MENTION THE CHALLENGE OF SOURCING OR MAKING FILM BIG ENOUGH TO FIT A CAMERA OF THIS SIZE.

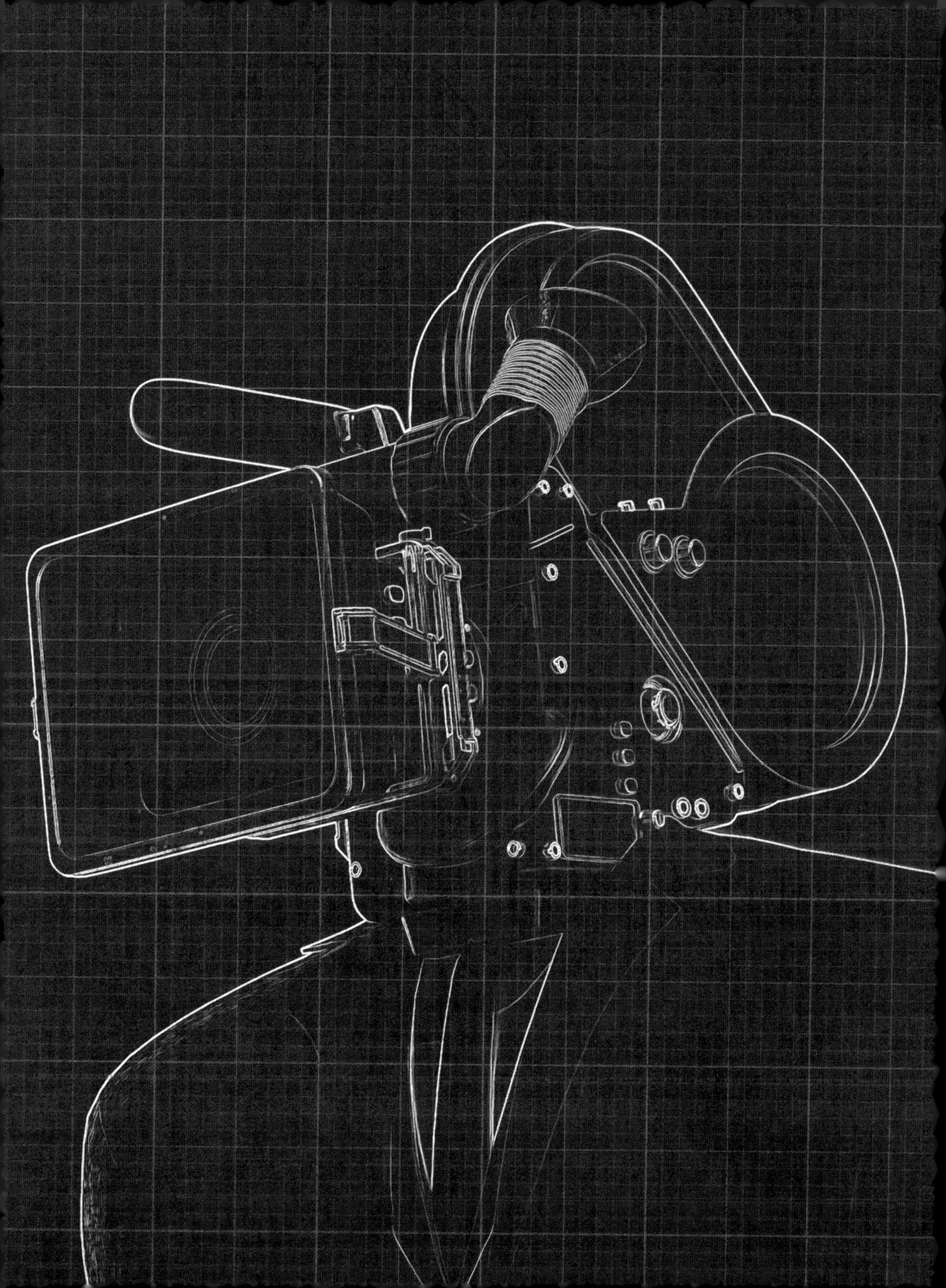

DETECTIVE CAMERAMAN

	SPECIES **CAMERAMAN**
	OCCUPATION **INVESTIGATOR**
	FACTION **CAMERA**
	HEIGHT **UNKNOWN**–MEDIUM

CRITICAL INFORMATION

BIT OF A CLICHÉ.

This elusive member of the Alliance isn't primarily geared toward combat operations. Instead he looks into mysteries and seeks evidence that might solve them. He wears a black fedora and a leather trench coat. He also carries a plasma revolver, a weapon no one else in the Alliance has—though he fires it only as a last resort, using it more as a threat.

The Alliance needs units like Detective Cameraman to investigate their own people, who may be working against them from within.

LESS OF A CLICHÉ.

A Cameraman who had taken part in many battles from the start of the war, surviving many brushes with death (files 46, 56, and 65), was arrested by Detective Cameraman due to suspicions he'd been covertly operating on the instructions of the Secret Agent (file 70). Detective Cameraman also conducted the interview of this Cameraman, confronting him with the evidence.

More recently, Detective Cameraman has been investigating the death of Plungerman, examining the remains of his body. Detective Cameraman's investigations have led to some tensions with other members of the Alliance, including a confrontation with Scientist TV Man. We need to make clear everyone should cooperate with Detective Cameraman's investigations: they're too important to be derailed.

CHIEF SCIENTIST CAMERAMAN

	SPECIES CAMERAMAN
	OCCUPATION ELITE SCIENTIST
	FACTION CAMERA 
	HEIGHT UNKNOWN–MEDIUM

CRITICAL INFORMATION

With the technology race against the enemy showing no signs of slowing down, the Alliance appointed a Cameraman to lead their scientific efforts (file 74). He has multiple cameras in addition to his head camera: one on each shoulder and another on his chest. (He has also been seen without the chest camera, and wearing a blue shirt as opposed to his white one.) Unlike other Scientist Cameramen, he doesn't wear a jacket and his robotic arms are visible.

FIELD RESEARCH

While the Chief Scientist's role is primarily focused on research and development, that doesn't mean he stays away from the front lines: He took part in the Siege of Alpha-Hills, and is on hand in the field to take samples of other tech for analysis (file 76). He and his team have an essential part to play in the conflict as it continues to unfold.

DRONE WARFARE

The Alliance's science corps are bolstered by the Camera Drones, which look similar to the head of a Large Cameraman (file 23). These operate in the field, and can make repairs to Alliance combatants such as Titan Cameraman. More recently these have been adapted to take part in battles, with lasers mounted on their sides.

TITAN CAMERAMAN

MAXIMUM THREAT LEVEL !

	SPECIES **CAMERAMAN**
	OCCUPATION **TITAN**
	FACTION **CAMERA** 
	HEIGHT **275 FEET** !!!

CRITICAL INFORMATION

The first Titan to be fielded by the Alliance (file 18), the Titan Cameraman has a similar CCTV head as his Normal counterpart's. In his original form, his most notable weapon was his core flame, which could be used to blast any enemy units directly in front of his blue reactor core: This was how he destroyed the Triple Skibidi Toilet (file 19). A laser fired from his finger wiped out several Normal Toilets (file 23).

Having been badly wounded in battle (file 20), Titan Cameraman was out of action for some considerable time before returning in upgraded form (file 50) with shoulder-mounted grenade cannons, a holographic shield, a gravity gun, a rail gun, and a mech hammer. He also wears a black leather trench coat and spiked brass knuckles. Unusual for a Cameraman, he does speak.

HE DOESN'T HAVE A LOT TO SAY, BUT WHEN HE DOES, HE SAYS IT LOUD.

RECOMMISSIONED

GLAD TO HAVE HIM BACK—HE'S ONE OF THE ALLIANCE'S MOST EFFECTIVE OPERATORS.

The upgraded Titan Cameraman returned to battle in style, destroying an army of Toilets that had attacked the Cameraman laboratory (file 50). He has continued to receive upgrades since then, which have equipped him with a buzzsaw arm, an acid blaster, and a detaining claw. He was one of the first Alliance members to take on an Astro Toilet (file 53).

THE SPEAKERMEN

	SPECIES **SPEAKERMAN**
	OCCUPATION **FOOT SOLDIER**
	FACTION **SPEAKER**
	HEIGHT **6 FEET 6 INCHES**

CRITICAL INFORMATION

OF COURSE.

Like the Cameramen, the Speakermen operate as ground troops against the Toilets. They have speakers for heads instead of cameras. They fight hand-to-hand, but can also use their speakers to perform sonic attacks against the Toilets. (The larger Speakermen are more effective at this, and so that tends to be their job.)

The Speakermen were deployed less in the war after the Titan Speakerman was compromised—but after his parasite was destroyed, they were able to return to the fray.

Needing something to counter the Toilets' relentless chant of their own anthem, the Speakermen were charged with broadcasting music. One track has become the Alliance's own victory song (file 24).

I DON'T KNOW WHERE THEY FOUND THE TRACK, BUT IT'S A GOOD CHOICE.

SPEAKERWOMAN

	**SPECIES** **SPEAKERMAN**
	**OCCUPATION** **ELITE FIGHTER**
	**FACTION** **SPEAKER**
	**HEIGHT** **6 FEET**

CRITICAL INFORMATION

Though she belongs to the Speakermen, Speakerwoman is very much her own person, with distinctive abilities (file 61). She can easily be spotted by the pink glow that comes from her speaker cone, which matches the pink elements in her otherwise black clothing. She has been known to associate with Camerawoman and TV Woman (file 66), and together the are an immensely effective team.

Speakerwoman's combat style is based around blades. She carries a pair of swords on her back and can shoot knives from positions mounted on the sides of her head, and uses her sound wave attack power to support this. Her most notable takedown was against a powerful toilet with unique light-based weaons (file 61). She has a relaxed vibe on the battlefield, dancing to music and mocking her opponents.

LEGENDARY MOMENT.

Interesting what the "official line" doesn't mention. I tried to offer Speakerwoman support after Dark Speakerman died, and she didn't want to know. I've never seen her so angry.

DARK SPEAKERMAN

	SPECIES SPEAKERMAN
	OCCUPATION INFILTRATOR
	FACTION SPEAKER
	HEIGHT UNKNOWN–MEDIUM

CRITICAL INFORMATI

Dark Speakerman is one of the Alliance's covert agents, identifiable by his glowing red speaker and matching red shirt (file 24). Like other Speakermen, he relies on knives as weapons, but is particularly skilled in their use. He has been a controversial figure among the Alliance due to his perceived ruthless nature. He focuses on his goals and permits no distractions.

DARK SPEAKERMAN WAS ANOTHER CASUALTY OF THE SIEGE OF ALPHA-HILLS (FILE 67).

CHIEF SCIENTIST TOILET RIPPED DARK SPEAKERMAN APART WITH HIS LASER (FILE 70). SOME CAMERAMEN MIGHT SAY HE GOT WHAT HE DESERVED, BECAUSE HIS ACTIONS DURING THAT MISSION LED TO THE DEATH OF TWO CAMERAMEN (FILE 69). HIS MISSION WAS THE DESTRUCTION OF THE CHIEF SCIENTIST, AND HE HELPED US GET THERE.

LARGE SPEAKERMEN

	**SPECIES** **SPEAKERMAN**
	**OCCUPATION** **SUPPORT UNITS**
	**FACTION**  **SPEAKER**
	**HEIGHT** **29 FEET**

CRITICAL INFORMATION

UNTIL YOU SEE ONE IN THE FLESH.

These larger variants of the Speakermen are even taller than Large Cameramen—they're some of the largest Alliance units outside the Titans. As well as being bigger than normal Speakermen, they differ in how they don't wear coats or suit jackets, instead wearing just shirts and pants.

Similar to the Large Cameramen, the Large Speakermen's main purpose is to support the attack, soaking up damage. Large Speakermen can use weaponry, as seen in the victory over the Berserker Skibidi Mutant (file 61), but they usually fight hand-to-hand. The Large Speakermen's strength is a huge asset on the battlefield. Their sound wave attacks can not only push back, disable, and confuse the enemy (file 37), they can also be used to eliminate obstacles such as locked doors (file 27).

THE FORCE OF A SOUND WAVE ATTACK CAN TURN A POTENTIAL DEFEAT INTO A RESOUNDING WIN.

TITAN SPEAKERMAN

MAXIMUM THREAT LEVEL !

	SPECIES **SPEAKERMAN**
	OCCUPATION **TITAN**
	FACTION **SPEAKER**
	HEIGHT **185 FEET**

CRITICAL INFORMATION

Titan Speakerman nearly won and lost the war for the Alliance. He looms large in history.

His giant stack of speakers allows him to make mighty sonic attacks. When he came onto the scene, the Alliance finally started to turn the tide against the Toilets. He was the one who defeated the Balaclava Skibidi Toilet (file 26).

But then the Toilets developed the Parasites. With these they could take over Alliance fighters and turn them against their comrades, which was bad enough. But taking control of a few Cameramen was never going to make that much difference, and the Toilets were always aiming for a bigger target. It took two Parasites—one to distract Titan Speakerman, one to infect him, but he has since been disinfected.

Under Toilet control (file 32), Titan Speakerman was used against the Alliance in several battles. They also upgraded him (file 57), including new arm-mounted plasma cannons and extra armor. During this time his core glowed yellow.

	SPECIES **TV MAN**
	OCCUPATION **SUPPORT TROOPS**
	FACTION **TV**
	HEIGHT **7 FEET 8 INCHES**

CRITICAL INFORMATION

The TV Men form the third main faction in the Alliance. They have television sets for heads, which are usually tuned to static, but they also display emoticons that can be used for communication, such as ◡̈ and ü—and they occasionally speak, too.

The TV Men's main weapons are their TV heads. With these they can shoot out a beam of hypnotizing light, which can stall an enemy long enough for others to strike (file 39). This was essential in defeating the Glitch Skibidi Toilet, who moved too fast to hit until he was hypnotized (file 54).

The TV Men can support the attack with melee combat, but they prefer not to—which has caused some tension between them and the Cameramen and Speakermen, who regularly put themselves in danger for the sake of the Alliance.

The TV Men are very effective at collecting information and technology, so that's where they're best deployed. They can connect to the feed of a Cameraman and display it, and they can teleport themselves and others. However, they sometimes value collecting technology more highly than the lives of their comrades, and have been known to abandon Cameramen in need of rescue because they wanted to focus on salvaging enemy tech.

The Toilets seem particularly scared of the TV Men, which in itself made the TV Men valuable allies when this was the focus of the war. In short, the TV Men are some of the most powerful fighters the Alliance has, but their main power is also their main weakness: If their screen is broken, their light is neutralized.

The TV Men's ability to teleport out of situations in a puff of black smoke is really useful for them, but it's hard to trust someone who could disappear at any moment and leave you to fend for yourself. However, they also use that teleport ability to jump in and save their comrades from certain death.

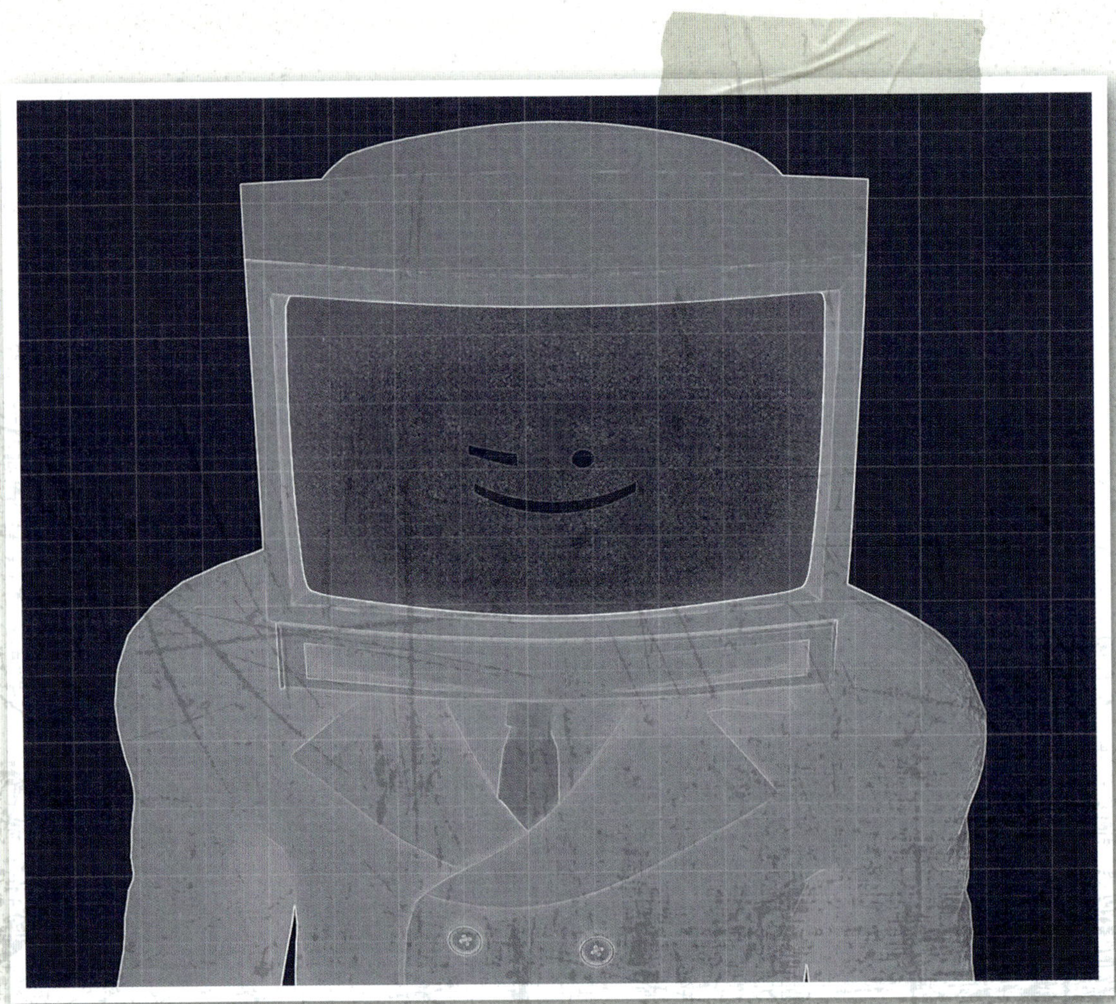

I sometimes wonder how far we can trust the TV Men. They can be very secretive, and I'm sure they keep information from us. They don't like to let Cameramen into their laboratory (File 74). It was also difficult to convince them to join forces with the Skibidi Toilets—their feud seems to run deep. If anything splits the Alliance, I think it will be the TV Men.

>w<

	**SPECIES** **TV MAN**
	**OCCUPATION** **ELITE AGENT**
	**FACTION** **TV**
	**HEIGHT** **8 FEET 1 INCH**

CRITICAL INFORMATION

One of the most powerful of the TV Men, and, therefore, one of the most powerful Alliance members full stop, TV Woman can be identified by her black coat, black boots, and 1960s-style TV head with a wooden cabinet. She often uses the >w< emoticon on her screen, but has also been seen to use -_- and Òwó.

TV Woman's ability to detach her head and operate it independently of her body, using small rockets to propel it, is valuable in the field of battle (file 49). Her TV is durable, surviving the explosion caused when she controlled the Flying Buzzsaw Toilet and crashed it into one of its comrades.

Mind Control

TV Woman's hypnosis not only freezes her victims, it also enables her to control them. As well as using her screen for attacks, she's guided Cameramen to safety with her light, and she has the rare ability to make fire attacks using her screen.

TV Woman has undergone upgrades to make herself an even more effective fighter in the field, including a jetpack, retractable knives, and shoulder spikes. She now has additional speakers fitted to the sides of her head, in addition to her built-in mono speaker.

She's more willing to get her hands dirty than most TV Men, and is a great asset to the Alliance. She has some big fans among the Cameramen, myself included.

TV Woman was part of the team that raided the Alpha-Hills Lab, fighting the Chief Scientist Toilet (file 70). She kept her cool after the death of Plungerman, and took on G-Toilet herself.

APEX™

Operating Instructions

Congratulations on your purchase of a new APEX™ television set. Please take a moment to familiarize yourself with these instructions before use.

- To turn the television ON, push the button at top right.
- To find channels, turn the dials.
- The UPPER dial can be used to tune into VHF band channels.
- The LOWER dial can be used to tune into UHF band channels.
- Note the position of favorite channels so you can easily find them again.
- If you experience problems getting a clear picture, try adjusting the position of the antennae on top of the cabinet.

*** If you see symbols and punctuation marks on the screen that seem to form facial expressions, please consult a qualified repairperson.**

>w<

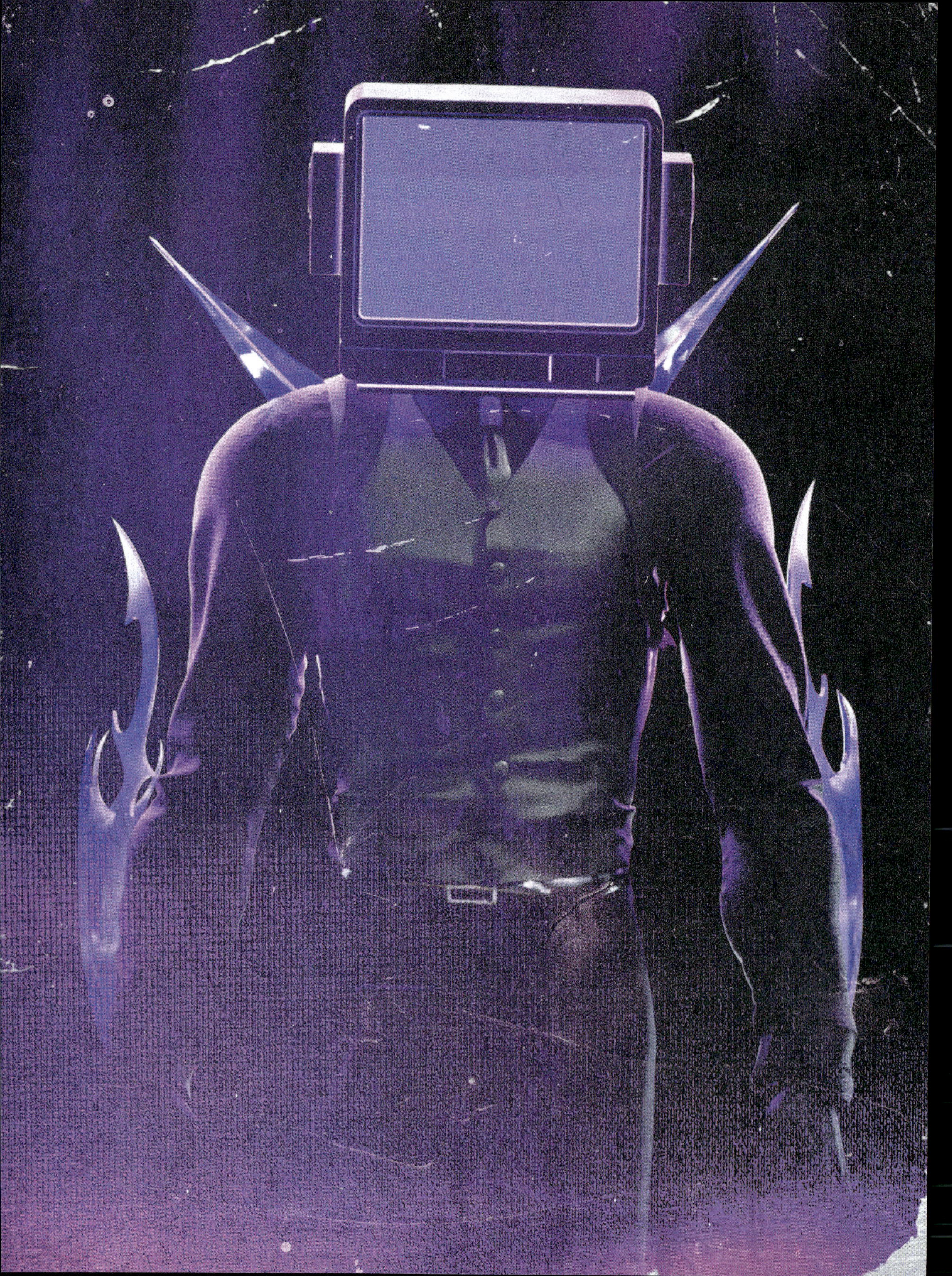

DARK TV MAN

	SPECIES	TV MAN
	OCCUPATION	ELITE AGENT
	FACTION	TV
	HEIGHT	8 FEET 1 INCH

CRITICAL INFORMATION

Dark TV Man can be identified by his purple screen and his overall purple glow. He's also stronger and more heavily armed than most other TV Men, with retractable blades in his arms and dual guns fitted to his head (file 73). And while most other TV Men avoid direct combat, Dark TV Man is a very skilled fighter capable of doing heavy damage.

As well as his built-in TV speakers, he has two further speakers, one on each side of his head. This enables him to combine sonic and visual attacks. If enemies try to use sunglasses to protect themselves against the hypnotizing TV light, the speakers can use sound waves to shatter these, exposing the victim's eyes and enabling the light to hit them (file 74).

Dark TV Man's hypnosis is more powerful than that of other TV Men, keeping the victim hypnotized for a time after the beam is turned off. He has also made use of a camera attachment, supplying footage from his POV (file 77). This means he has the abilities of a Cameraman and a Speakerman, in addition to being a TV Man. A real triple threat.

Dark TV Man can also use his teleportation ability in unusual and powerful ways. He can bring objects directly to his hands—for example, decapitating a Toilet by making its head appear in his hand. He can also deflect attacks by creating a portal in one hand that absorbs the attack, then sending it to his other hand so he can redirect it wherever he chooses.

Like other TV Men, he speaks—but everything he says is reversed. So if you want to understand him, you have to think backward.

DARK TV MAN IS UNDOUBTEDLY AN ELITE ALLIANCE FIGHTER. HIS SKILLS HELPED US ESCAPE FROM ALPHA-HILLS (FILE 73), BUT HE IS ANOTHER ONE WE SHOULD WATCH CAREFULLY.

I BELIEVE HIS FIRST LOYALTY IS TO THE TV MEN, RATHER THAN THE GREATER GOOD OF THE ALLIANCE, AND HE SUPPLIES THE TV MEN WITH MUCH OF THEIR INTEL.

".nettor era sniarb riehT"

DARK TV MAN, ON THE INFECTED HUMANS

NOTABLY HE IS SUBSERVIENT TO SCIENTIST TV MAN, WHO I AM NOT CONVINCED WE CAN TRUST. HE CERTAINLY CONCEALS INFORMATION, EVEN FROM OTHER TV MEN, AND MANY OF HIS ACTIONS HAVE INVOLVED THE COLD-BLOODED SACRIFICE OF ALLIANCE FIGHTERS.

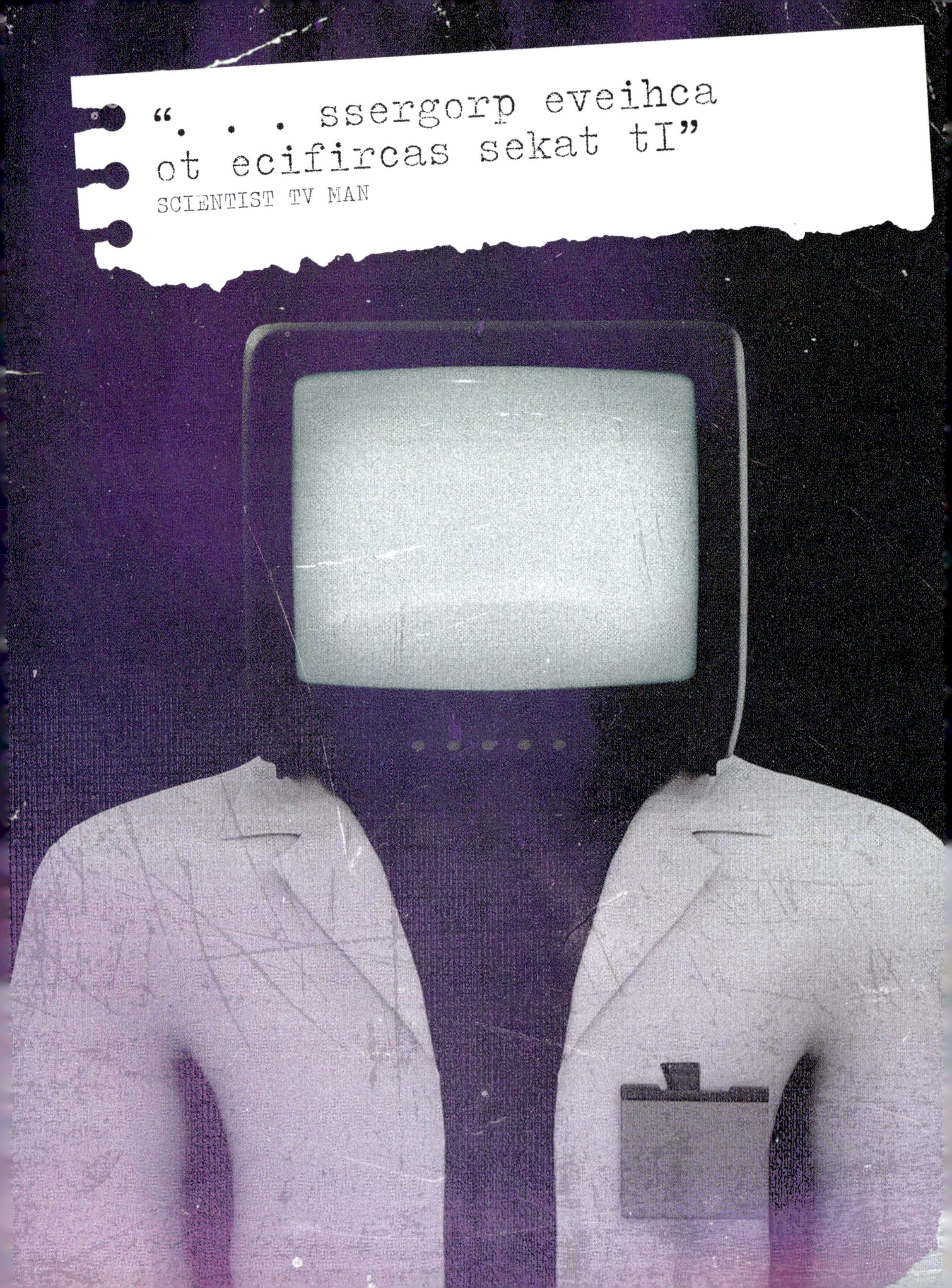
". . . ssergorp eveihca
ot ecifircas sekat tI"
SCIENTIST TV MAN

SCIENTIST TV MAN

	**SPECIES** **TV MAN**
	**OCCUPATION** **ELITE SCIENTIST**
	**FACTION** **TV**
	**HEIGHT** **UNKNOWN**–MEDIUM

CRITICAL INFORMATION

LIKES HOW IT LOOKS.

The Scientist TV Man occupies a very significant position in the TV Men's hierarchy, as you'd expect from the TV Men's heavy focus on tech. He looks somewhat similar to other TV Men, but he has a wire aerial attached to his TV head (and it's round, rather than the two-pronged version sported by TV Woman). It's unknown whether this serves any purpose. He wears a white coat (file 66).

In keeping with the often secretive attitude of the TV Men, the Scientist TV Man dislikes any recording being made in his laboratory, demanding Dark TV Man turn off his camera in there (file 74). And like other TV Men, he speaks backward to make himself difficult for non-TV Men to understand—though he has spoken to human survivors using a translator that reverses his voice.

I WONDER WHAT HE MIGHT BE HIDING. MAYBE SOMETHING TO DO WITH HIS ACTIVITIES BEFORE JOINING THE ALLIANCE . . .

	**SPECIES** TV MAN
	**OCCUPATION** REINFORCEMENT SQUAD
	**FACTION** TV
	**HEIGHT** UNKNOWN–VERY LARGE

CRITICAL INFORMATION

The attack capabilities of TV Men increase with size, and so Large TV Man's attacks are more powerful than those of normal TV Men. In his original form his screen was fitted to a flexible mount, and he was equipped with four extra TV screens in addition to his head screen (file 40), but a later upgrade replaced these extra TVs with speakers, allowing him to attack in quadrophonic sound (file 68).

A further upgrade increased his size, replacing the speakers with detaining claws and adding extra TV screens on the sides of his head, which is no longer fitted on a mount (file 77). These screens further enhance his attacks. He's also fitted with a screen protector to keep his screen from being cracked in battle.

When the Skibidi Toilets used their sunglasses to protect themselves from the TV Men's rays, Large TV Man retreated with the rest of his fellow TV Men (File 43). But he also rescued a group of Alliance fighters from the Buzzsaw Mutant (File 66), and went to the forefront of the battle against the Chief Scientist Toilet, taking the brunt of the attack (File 70).

	**SPECIES** TV MAN
	**OCCUPATION** TITAN
	**FACTION** TV
	**HEIGHT** 235 FEET

CRITICAL INFORMATION

Titan TV Man is a tank-style fighter, with good hand-to-hand combat skills and the ability to take high levels of damage—but his slow movement and reaction times can leave him vulnerable to attack. He has the same teleportation ability as other TV Men, which, when paired with his ability to fly, allows him to move across battlefields surprisingly quickly.

His claws can be used in melee combat, and he also has grappling hooks that can draw and hold enemies while he uses his signature move, the Death Screen. Only he can do this, and it involves projecting a red screen at the target. The victim is hypnotized and can't control themself anymore. Larger enemies have some resistance against the Death Screen, but even then it often has some effect: For example, it took away G-Toilet's laser-eye ability.

With the addition of large speakers, Titan TV Man became Cinemaman, with the ability to use sonic attacks to destroy the eyewear used by the Toilets to protect themselves from the TV

Men's attacks. In this form he was crucial in fighting back against Infected Titan Speakerman, though he eventually took a knife to the screen and had to retreat.

Titan TV Man was repaired and returned in upgraded form (file 66). This version is considered the most powerful fighter the Alliance has ever fielded.

The upgraded Titan TV Man has three head-mounted TVs, which he can detach and operate independently in a similar way to TV Woman (file 68). He has two additional shoulder-mounted TVs and a further torso-mounted TV, and his reactor core emits an energy beam. He wields a retractable energy blade and can make dive attacks, in which he flies toward the target and aims to knock them down.

Titan TV Man made some important early strikes in the battle with the Astro Toilets (files 70, 71, and 73), and while he sustained a series of injuries, his function was not significantly impaired. After repairs he was fitted with a shield projector and a hidden detaining claw (file 77). After a gruelling solo battle with several Astro Toilets, he faced off against the Juggernaut, stealing its shock wave cannon and attaching it to himself.

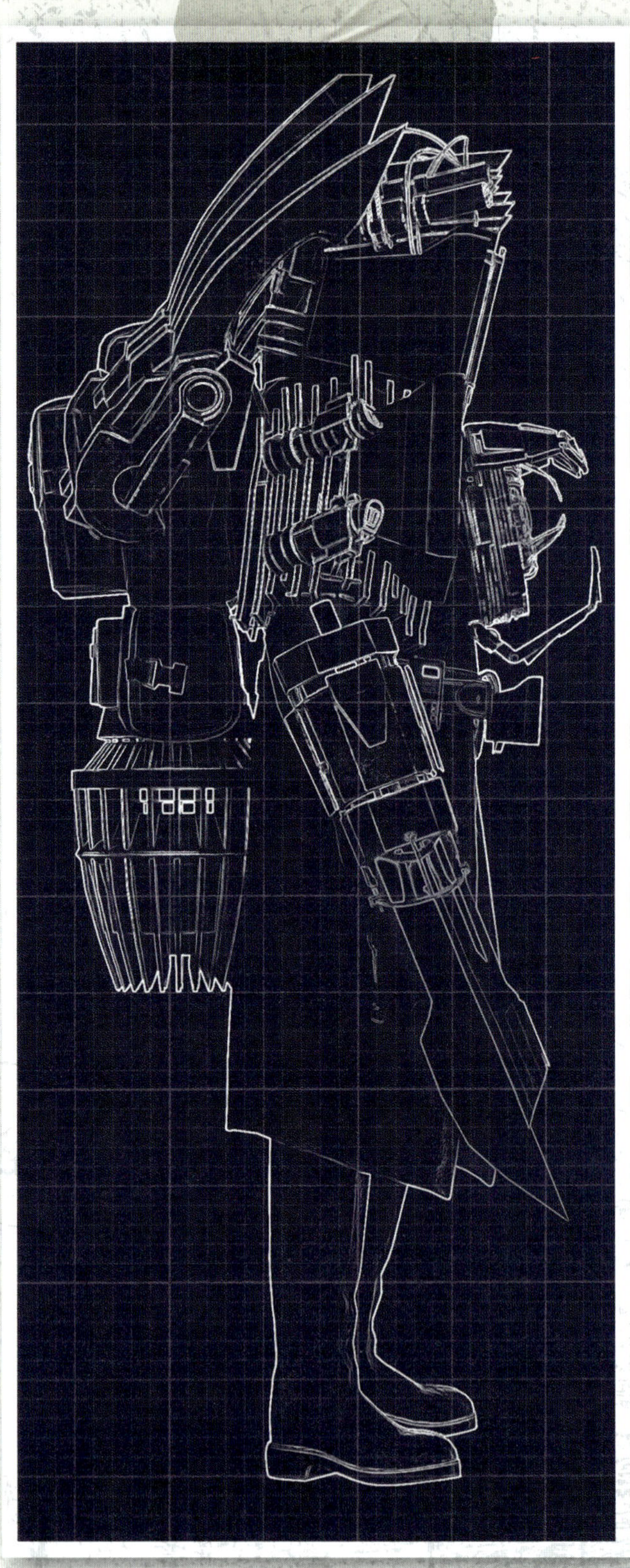

Titan TV Man would have died in this fight if not for the intervention of G-Toilet, but he was later captured and corrupted by the Astro Toilets and transformed into the Watchman of Doom.

OTHERS

There are other figures who have some part to play in this war. Some are humans who lived on Earth before the war began, and may have taken on a different form to fight in it. There's also a faction that seems determined to influence the war, but it's not clear how they want to influence the war, or what outcome they're looking for. They seem to be on the side of the Alliance—but given the shady way they operate, it's hard to be sure . . .

I found some human survivors at Alpha-Hills who'd managed to hide out while the war raged on (File 73). Thankfully I managed to communicate to them that I was a friend. Everyone knows what a thumbs-up means. The more we can locate, the better.

If any humans are reading this, keep your headphones on at all times. Noise-cancelling ones are best. And put some good music on. It won't keep you from getting killed, but it'll make you feel better about the whole situation.

SECRET AGENT

	SPECIES HUMAN?
	OCCUPATION SECRET AGENT
	FACTION OTHER
	HEIGHT 6 FEET 3 INCHES

WE KNOW FAR TOO LITTLE ABOUT THIS GUY.

CRITICAL INFORMATION

Secret Agent looks human, but we don't know for sure. He wears a suit and sunglasses, and he likes to keep in the background. He was first spotted in footage we'd captured, seemingly just observing (file 45). However, further incidents revealed he seems to be manipulating events from the sidelines, but why?

He used to work at Alpha-Hills Labs, which is maybe how he gained some of his special abilities, like teleportation and telepathy.

Some say he can survive bursts of fire. He can certainly hack into technology, interfering with head functions. He's been an ally so far but nobody can afford to trust him.

ANY OPERATIVE WHO SEES THE SECRET AGENT, REGARDLESS OF WHAT HE'S DOING, SHOULD REPORT BACK. EVERY DETAIL. ANY LITTLE THING MAY HELP US.

GREEN CAMERAMEN

SPECIES
HUMAN?

OCCUPATION
INFILTRATOR

FACTION

CAMERA

HEIGHT
UNKNOWN—NORMAL

CRITICAL INFORMATION

Two Cameramen with green detailing on their suits joined the Infiltration Squad for the Alpha-Hills operation (file 67). These two were seemingly killed by the toilets after having the doors closed on them by Dark Speakerman (file 69)—however, they were subsequently repaired and returned to service. They display unusual green lights and can phase through solid objects. We now know these Cameramen work for the Secret Agent, and presumably have been relaying information about the Alliance's activities back to him.

THEY'RE NOT THE ONLY ONES.

USUALLY YOU SEE ONLY TWO OF THE GREEN CAMERAMEN AT ONCE, BUT A THIRD HAS DEFINITELY BEEN SEEN ON OCCASION. I DON'T KNOW FOR SURE HOW MANY THERE ARE.

MISSION UNKNOWN

It is possible that the Green Cameramen were placed on the Infiltration Squad to ensure the group achieved its mission and didn't go off-brief. There are no records detailing when and how they were recruited, though we suspect the Shapeshifter was responsible. But they can be helpful to the Alliance, and the Alliance needs all the help it can get.

SHAPESHIFTER AGENT

SPECIES

HUMAN ?

OCCUPATION

INFILTRATOR

FACTION

CAMERA

HEIGHT

UNKNOWN-NORMAL

CRITICAL INFORMATION

This human is presumed to be part of the Secret Agent's collective, not least because her green attire matches that of other members of the group (file 75). The Shapeshifter makes use of hologram projection to disguise herself. Known disguises used by the Shapeshifter include a car, a chair, and a potted palm tree (file 77).

The source of the Shapeshifter's powers is unclear. As well as her holograms, she can fly without the use of a jetpack and can ram enemies at high speeds without damaging herself, suggesting she is more than human. It's possible that the green core she wears at her neck grants her these abilities.

The Shapeshifter is to be treated with maximum caution. She appears to act as a recruiter for the Secret Agent, installing a program called alpha_hills_OS, which brings operatives into the collective (file 77). If you see her, do not allow her to come near you.

Theories that the Shapeshifter is able to hack Cameramen, causing them to see other objects in place of her, have proved to be wide of the mark. Her holograms are visible to everyone, including humans.

THE ASTRO TOILETS

The timing couldn't have been worse for the Alliance. The raid on the Skibidi Toilets' stronghold at Alpha-Hills Labs had been grueling and the cost had been high—but it had been successful. The place where all their technology was developed had fallen to the Alliance, and the Chief Scientist Toilet was dead. It's possible the Alliance could have won the war from there . . .

But then the Astro Toilets turned the war on its head. They'd been around for a while (file 51), initially providing support to the Skibidi Toilets (files 53 and 55), before losing patience with G-Toilet's failures such as the Alliance's disinfection of Titan Speakerman (file 57). The Astro Toilets attempted to assassinate G-Toilet (file 60), then broke off ties with the Skibidi Toilets, deciding to take Earth for themselves. And it wouldn't be the first planet they've taken by force.

THE BAD NEWS IS THE ASTROS ARE MORE TECHNOLOGICALLY ADVANCED THAN THE SKIBIDI FACTION, AS WELL AS BEING STRATEGICALLY SMARTER AND HARDER TO KILL. DEFEATING THEM IS GOING TO BE AN EVEN BIGGER CHALLENGE FOR THE ALLIANCE—EVEN WITH THE SKIBIDI TOILETS ON THEIR SIDE . . .

TROOP ASTRO TOILET

	SPECIES **ASTRO TOILET**
	OCCUPATION **RANK-AND-FILE**
	FACTION **ASTRO**
	HEIGHT **UNKNOWN**–MEDIUM

CRITICAL INFORMATION

This seems to be the Astro equivalent of Normal Skibidi Toilets—they're certainly the most common type of Astro Toilet and the lowest ranking as seen by the lack of stripes on their helmets (file 76). They have similar X-shaped wings as the Obliterators, and two small levitators mounted on their backs. Instead of a cistern, they have a battery pack that charges their twin plasma blasters.

THE ASTROS SEEM HAPPY TO THROW THE TROOPS INTO BATTLE TO BE WIPED OUT IF IT GAINS THEM A TACTICAL ADVANTAGE. HOWEVER, THE TROOPS ARE NOT TO BE UNDERESTIMATED: THEY CAN CREATE CHAOS WITH THEIR SONIC CHARGE ABILITY (FILE 76).

Be ready with holographic shields to protect against the sonic charges. And don't assume they're downed because they've been stabbed in the head, either (file 77). They seem to have some way of reviving themselves after what should be a critical injury.

While the Troops were initially more powerful than their counterparts in the ranks of the Alliance and the Skibidi Toilets, we've worked on upgrades that should enable our people to hold their own.

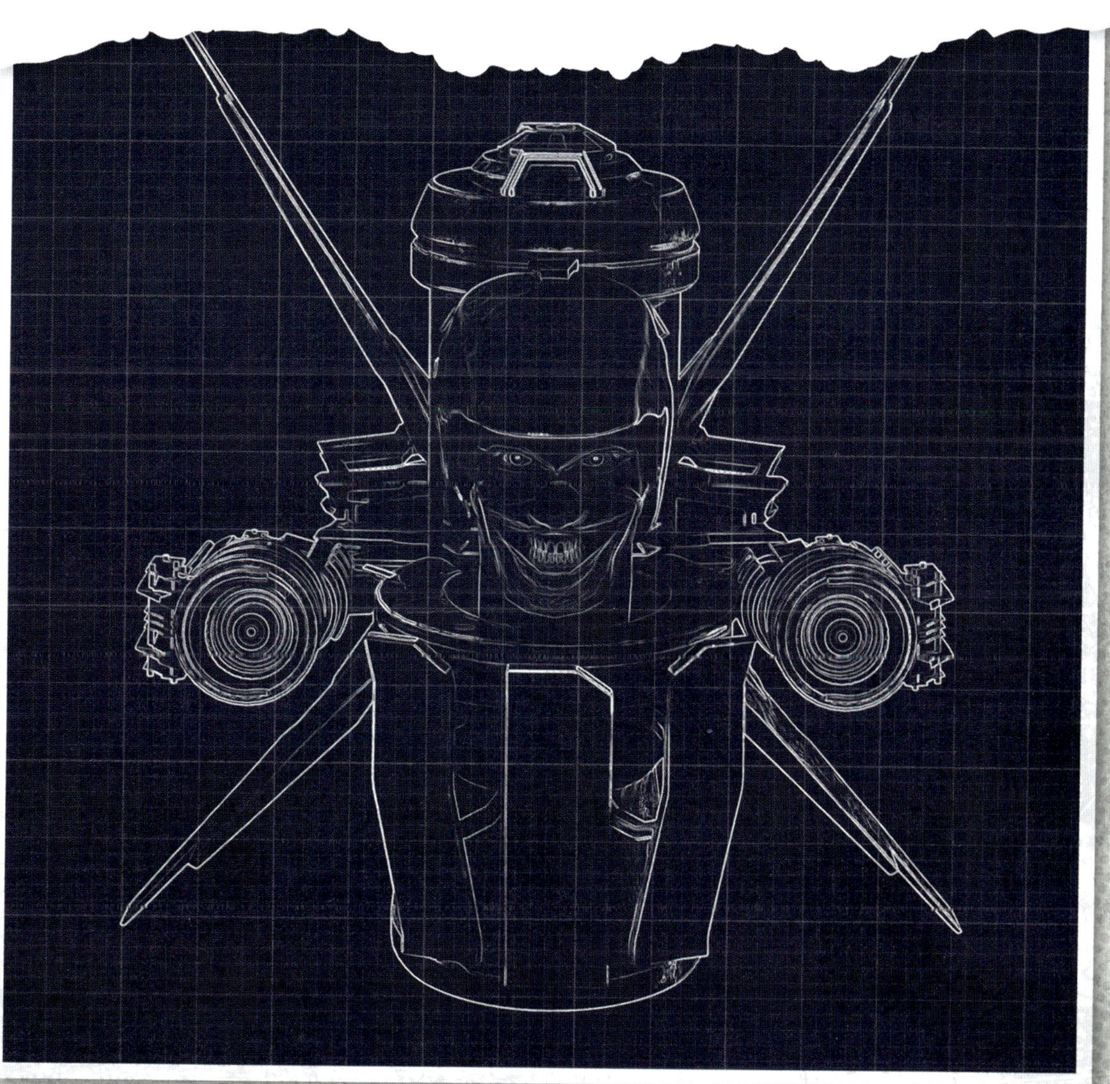

DETAINER ASTRO TOILET

	SPECIES **ASTRO TOILET**
	OCCUPATION **FOOT SOLDIER**
	FACTION **ASTRO**
	HEIGHT **UNKNOWN**–MEDIUM?

CRITICAL INFORMATION

The Detainer Astro Toilet is pretty much second-in-command to the Assailant, although he's a lot bigger (you couldn't shut his lid, his head's too big). WHAT WOULD HAPPEN IF YOU TRIED TO FLUSH HIM?

He has the same warp-speed ability, but he also has claws—one on each side and a third that extends over his head. The claws can be used to grab opponents, and one of them has a retractable blade for powerful melee attacks. He wears a helmet—the stripes on the top indicate his rank.

He used his claws to hold G-Toilet while the Assailant moved in to strike the killer blow—but the Chief Scientist Toilet joined the fray and cut off one of the claws (File 60).

WHEN THE DETAINER CAME BACK, REPAIRED AND UPGRADED (FILE 70), THEY HAD FITTED HIM WITH THREE NEW, ENHANCED CLAWS, WHICH CAN CRUSH OPPONENTS USING WAVES OF ENERGY.

The Interceptors have one other tactic we must all watch out for: if downed, they will emit their self-destruct scream and then explode (File 77). The purpose of this is twofold: it can take out any survivors while also avoiding their technology falling into enemy hands. Don't go near an Interceptor unless you're certain it's dead. I recommend a sniper shot to ensure it's finished off.

INTERCEPTOR ASTRO TOILETS

	SPECIES **ASTRO TOILET**
	OCCUPATION **STRIKE FORCE**
	FACTION **ASTRO**
	HEIGHT **UNKNOWN**–LARGE

CRITICAL INFORMATION

The Interceptors are similar to attack planes, small enough to be quick and maneuverable but large enough to pack a punch (file 74). They operate particularly well in air-to-air combat, and have taken down the Alliance's camera helicopters (file 75). They will crash into the enemy head-on, with little concern for their own safety, and seem to take great pleasure in the carnage they cause.

DANGEROUS ARMAMENTS

Interceptors are equipped with rapid-fire plasma cannons: These are relatively low-powered and low-accuracy, so their attacks often involve passing the target at high speed while firing continuously, making a hit more likely and making it difficult for the target to retaliate. When engaging an Interceptor in combat, it's important to keep moving: It thrives against slow targets (file 75).

DESTRUCTOR ASTRO TOILETS

	SPECIES ASTRO TOILET
	OCCUPATION ASSAULT UNITS
	FACTION ASTRO
	HEIGHT UNKNOWN—GIANT

CRITICAL INFORMATION

The Destructors are heavily armored Astro Toilets equipped with masked helmets that also feature an energy shield. This protects their heads from damage (file 74). Their main weapons are twin gravity-gun lasers, one mounted on each side of the toilet, but they're also equipped with four plasma cannons.

EXTRA RAM CAPACITY

The Destructors can transform into a more compact shape that enables them to ram opponents with greater force and with lower risk of damage to themselves. In this mode, their lasers are reversed to function as thrusters, giving them greater speed and impact (file 77).

THE DESTRUCTORS ARE VERY CHALLENGING ENEMIES, BUT THEY CAN BE DEFEATED IN THE FIELD: ONE OF THEM FACED OFF WITH TITAN TV MAN AND LOST (FILE 77).

Despite their speed and power, it's possible to distract a Destructor long enough to make a critical attack, and in one memorable case the distraction was provided by a Cameraman called Fred. This guy came back from infection to fight for the Alliance, but at the time of writing I don't know what his condition is.

So while Obliterators are relatively low-ranking Astros, eliminating one is a very valuable thing to do—it may destroy further Astros getting a ride. Watch the video of the battle in New York City if you want to see how one was defeated by a group of Skibidi Toilets: laser fire concentrated on the head seems effective (file 76).

OBLITERATOR ASTRO TOILETS

	SPECIES **ASTRO TOILET**
	OCCUPATION **RANK-AND-FILE**
 	FACTION **ASTRO**
	HEIGHT **UNKNOWN**–TITAN

CRITICAL INFORMATION

The first Astro Toilets to be seen on Earth were large flying Astros with limited weaponry (file 51). The fact the Astros didn't send anything more powerful suggests at that point they didn't think Earth was that important, or didn't expect to encounter heavy resistance. Once things got serious, they started sending Obliterators instead—larger and much better armed Astros (file 74).

Obliterators can be identified by their X-shaped mechanical wings, though they also have two larger main wings, each of which is fitted with two plasma cannons. They're willing to bite and ram opponents. They may be used as bodyguards for high-ranking Astro Toilets (file 77), and also act as troop transports for smaller Astros such as Troopers, Striders, and Specialists.

ASSAILANT ASTRO TOILET

	SPECIES **ASTRO TOILET**
	OCCUPATION **OVERSEER**
	FACTION **ASTRO**
	HEIGHT **19–59 FEET**

CRITICAL INFORMATI…

Saw a new type of Toilet on the battlefield—whole new design. Large but not giant. Black toilet and it wears a helmet. Technologically advanced, it has a ring around it and a photon cannon fitted to its base. It warped into battle, killed a large Speakerman. I was gonna fight it myself, but when the Titan Cameraman arrived, it warped out again. Watch out for more of these. Seems like a new evolution maybe (File 53).

UPDATE

This guy turned up again, getting into a confrontation with G-Toilet, or we thought it was G-Toilet (in fact, it was a decoy). There was an exchange in their language, which got more and more heated. Another Toilet joined them and they tried to take down the decoy. They failed, then warped out of there. Toilets fighting Toilets. What's happening? Have they split into factions? Number ones and number twos (File 60)?

OLD ENEMIES

The Assailant Astro Toilet is a commander of the Astro faction. There's bad blood between him and G-Toilet, and we think they knew each other before coming to Earth. The confrontation between them was the moment the war turned on its head.

WARP CAPABILITIES

Like other Astro Toilets, the Assailant uses a Static Warp Levitator to travel, eliminating the need for a jetpack or rotor and enabling movement at very high speed (file 53). It can be supercharged for even higher power.

HIERARCHY

Observations of the Astro hierarchy suggest that while the Assailant is an important and high-ranking figure in the military, he is seemingly outranked by the Duchess Astro Toilet, whose attacks include lasers shooting from her eyes and mouth. She has since taken on an upgraded Titan form with a humanoid body.

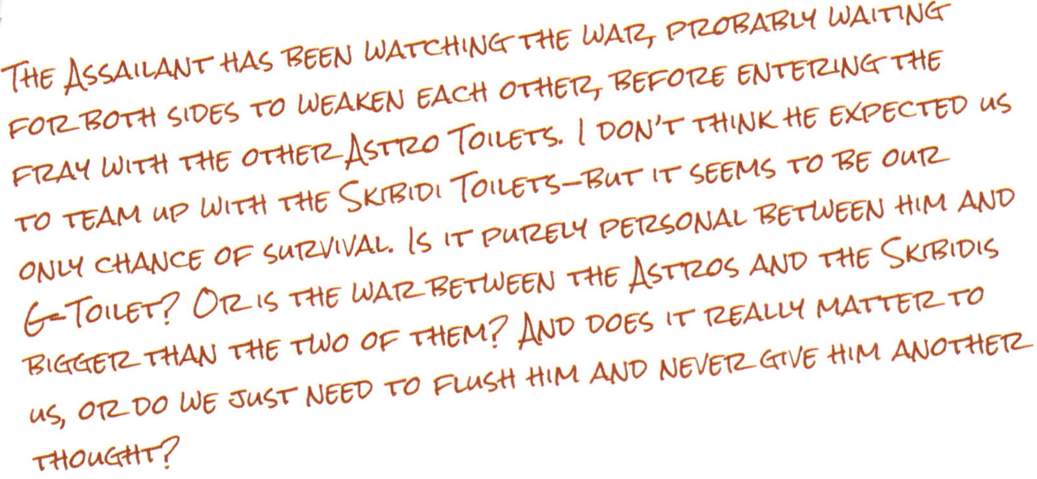

JUGGERNAUT ASTRO TOILET

	SPECIES ASTRO TOILET
	OCCUPATION TITAN
	FACTION ASTRO
	HEIGHT UNKNOWN–BIG

CRITICAL INFORMATION

A huge, heavily armed Astro, with an appearance obviously designed to look menacing—three spikes on his helmet and two mechanical arms. He carries a shockwave cannon and an energy shield.

He's powerful enough to beat Titan Speakerman in battle (File 72). He destroyed an entire mountain range (File 77).

Perhaps surprisingly, the Juggernaut seems to have more complex emotional reactions than other Toilets, most of whom seem driven by anger, pleasure in destruction, and singing. An example of this came when we killed his comrade,

THE SCOUT ASTRO TOILET (WHICH RESEMBLES A SMALLER VERSION OF HIM—THE JUGGERNAUT SCREAMED WHEN THE SCOUT WAS HIT, AND SEEMED TO REGARD THE SCOUT AS HIS SON). THE JUGGERNAUT SEEMED TO STOP AND GRIEVE. IF ANYTHING, I THINK THIS MAKES HIM MORE DANGEROUS, AS HE WILL BECOME MORE MOTIVATED TO SEEK REVENGE ON US.

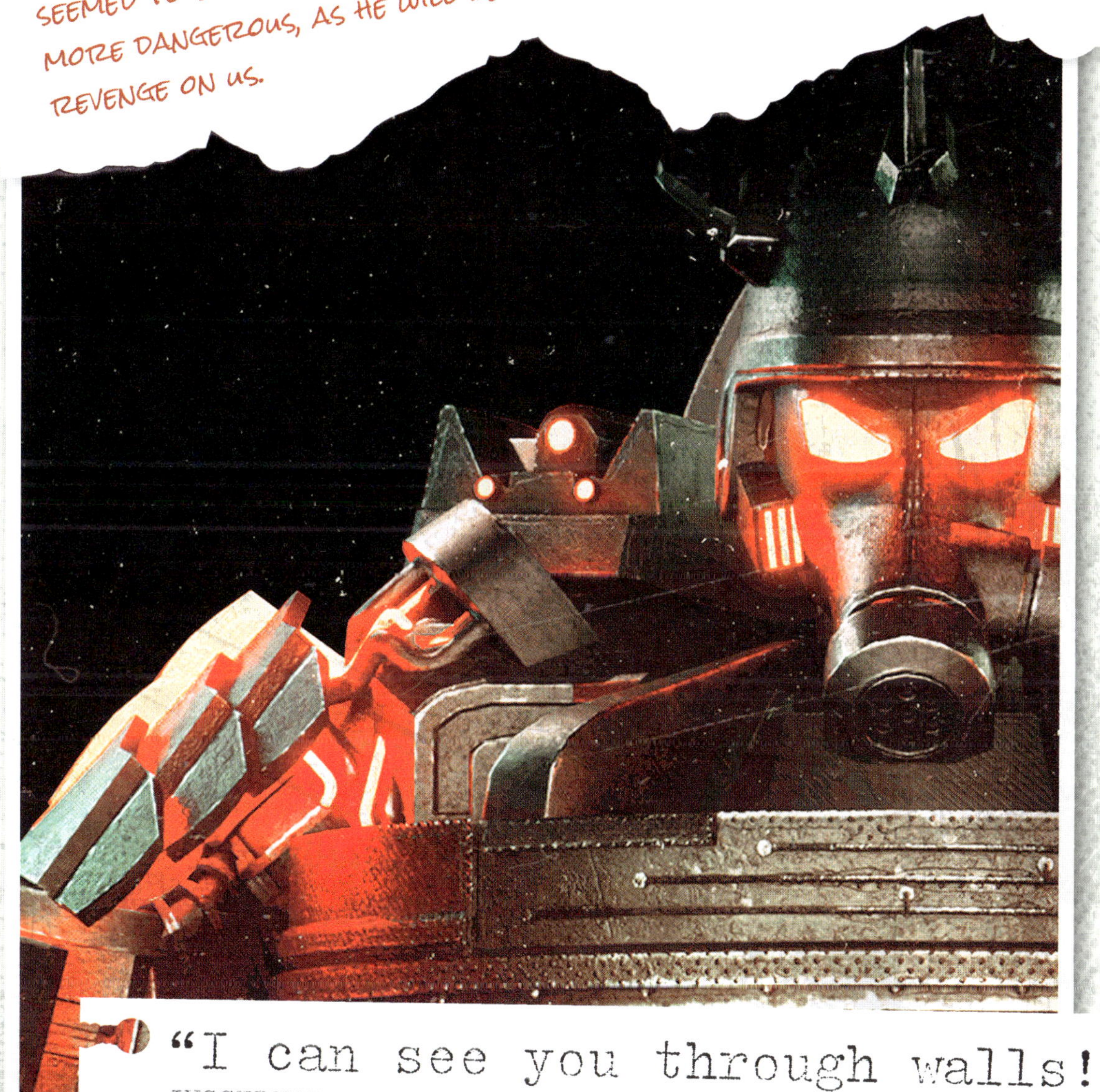

"I can see you through walls!"
JUGGERNAUT ASTRO TOILET

MOTHERSHIP ASTRO TOILET

	SPECIES **ASTRO TOILET**
	OCCUPATION **ELITE SUPPORT**
	FACTION **ASTRO**
	HEIGHT **UNKNOWN**—COLOSSAL

CRITICAL INFORMATION

The largest participant in the war so far, the Mothership Astro Toilet is . . . well, pretty much what he sounds like. He's a living transporter for the Astros, which also serves as a base and repair station, as well as being heavily armed in his own right (file 74). His main weapon is a plasma cannon fitted to his underside, which is powerful enough to destroy mountains (file 77). He can also call on a plasma shield that protects him from damage.

The Mothership's size and weight make him relatively slow, and any movement for him takes up a lot of energy—including warping, which requires a long charge-up. Additionally, there are warning signs before he warps in.

WHAT DOES HE NEED THAT SHIELD FOR? HE'S SO HUGE, MOST OF OUR ATTACKS DON'T SEEM TO REGISTER WITH HIM. FOR HIM, GETTING SHOT BY ONE OF OUR WEAPONS MUST BE LIKE BEING HEAD-BUTTED BY AN ANT.

SEEING ORANGE?

If you see an orange warp effect in the air above you, alert all other units in the area

IMMEDIATELY

THE MOTHERSHIP IS ON ITS WAY.

EARLY WARNING COULD SAVE LIVES!

DUCHESS ASTRO TOILET

	SPECIES **ASTRO TOILET**
	OCCUPATION **ELITE**
	FACTION **ASTRO**
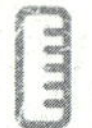	HEIGHT **UNKNOWN**–TITAN

CRITICAL INFORMATION

One of the highest-ranking Astro Toilets, the Duchess is also the only female Astro we currently know of. She was first encountered as a giant Astro form (file 76), equipped with four tendrils, each fitted with a laser turret, alongside her eye and mouth lasers. Her incredible strength was demonstrated in an encounter with Alliance forces, as she destroyed the Rocketeer Skibidi Mutant. Even though the poor guy had surrendered.

UPDATES

The Duchess has since been upgraded into Titan form with a humanoid body (file 77). As with her previous form, and unlike all other Astro Toilets, she doesn't wear a helmet: In its place she has a huge red halo-type construction that floats around her head, which rotates at greater speed the more energy she uses. Her Titan form also features a huge static warp levitator of similar design to the halo.

WEAPONRY

The Titan Duchess has a new signature weapon in the form of a plasma whip, which can attack enemies at considerable range, and her laser tendrils have been enhanced into tentacles. Both weapons were used in her capture of Titan TV Man, after which her sadistic side came out: She inflicted pain on him for fun, then infected him.

The war has raged across the entire world—here are some of the locations where key events took place. One thing's for sure: No one ever complains about the lack of public toilets in these places anymore . . .

DUBAI

The battle where Titan Speakerman was finally disinfected happened here—a dangerous place to fight, given it contains some of Earth's largest buildings (file 57).

LONDON

The UK capital was severely damaged by the Skibidi Toilet occupation, with Big Ben being repurposed as a laser emplacement. After getting a significant upgrade, Titan Speakerman battled the Toilets here (file 59).

MIAMI

The Alliance—including Speakerwoman—battled the Skibidi Toilet armed with light weapons here (file 61).

ALPHA-HILLS LABS

This research facility was built by humans, but was taken over by the Skibidi Toilets, who installed their own Toilet production line and developed new weapons and other tech there. The Alliance launched a major assault, infiltrated Alpha-Hills, and took control (files 66–74).

NEW YORK CITY

After a coordinated effort, the Alliance liberated New York from the Skibidi Toilets—a major victory that seemed to signal the Alliance had the upper hand (file 53). However, it was later the site of a battle with Astro Toilets that ended with the destruction of the city (file 76).

DENVER

This city in Colorado was the site of another face-off with the Astro Toilets, as the upgraded Cameramen entered the fray (file 77).

VEHICLES AND TECH

The story of this war has been an escalation of technology on both sides. When it started, the Skibidi Toilets made only limited use of technology. But the Alliance developed equipment to protect themselves and weapons to strike back, and the Skibidi Toilets raised their own technology game in return. They often took the Alliance's tech, modifying it and using it against them . . . and now the Astro Toilets are more advanced still.

THIS ISN'T A RUNDOWN OF EVERY PIECE OF TECH USED BY EITHER SIDE DURING THE COURSE OF THE WAR—THERE ARE FAR TOO MANY TO LIST—BUT IT INCLUDES DETAILS OF SOME OF THE MORE SIGNIFICANT ONES. HOPEFULLY SOME OF THIS STUFF CAN, ONE DAY, BE USED TO REBUILD THE WORLD INSTEAD OF FIGHT OVER IT . . .

HARVESTING PROTOCOL

On the battlefield, survival is the most important thing. Ensure the safety of yourselves and your comrades before anything else.

Bodies of enemies will be picked up by specialist harvesting squads. Mark any bodies on the map for them to find.

Pick up any weaponry or other portable tech you can find. Nothing should be wasted! Just check that it's not booby-trapped and is about to self-destruct.

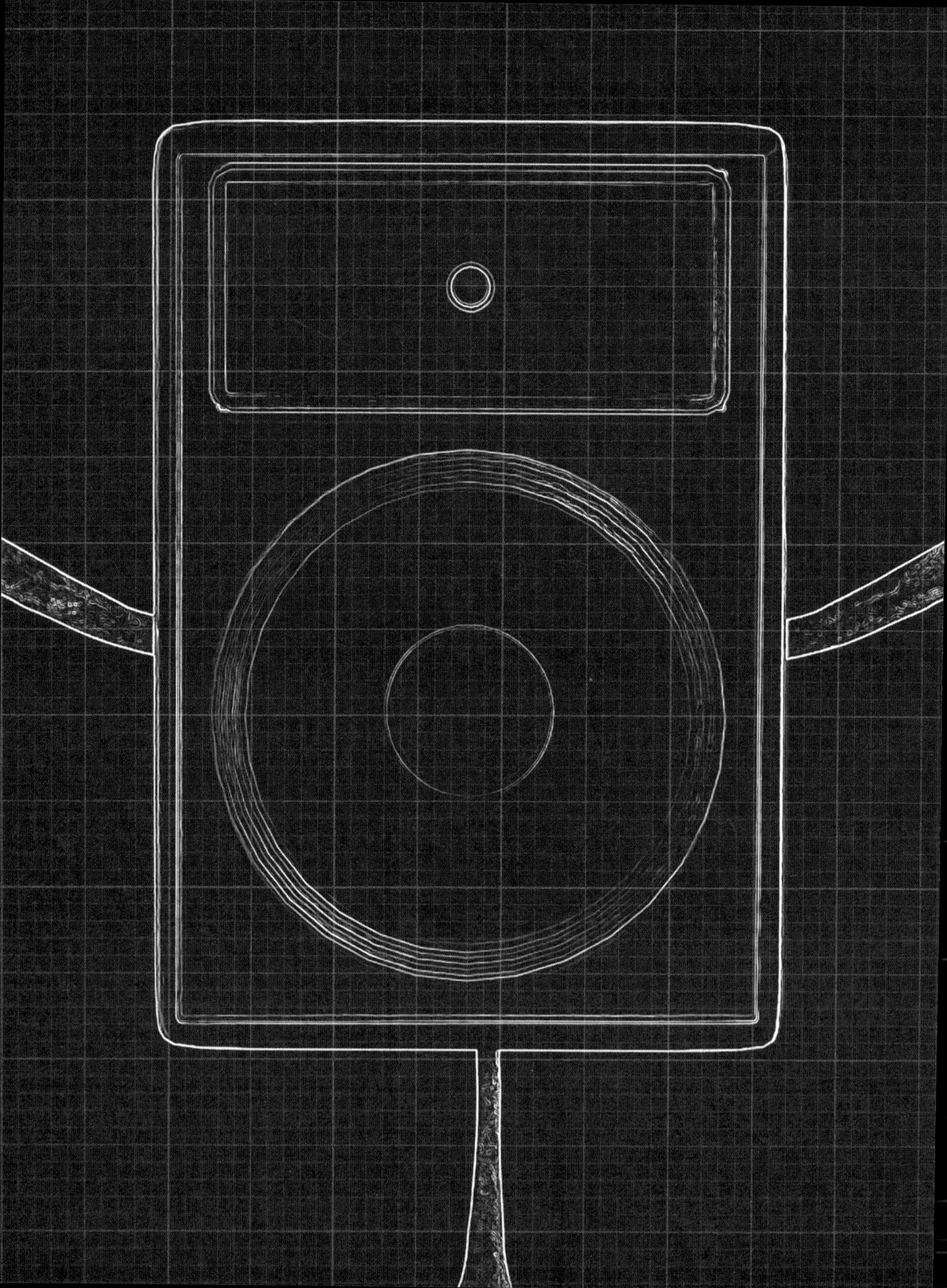

STRIDERS

IF YOU GET THEM TO TURN THE VOLUME DOWN A LITTLE, THE TRACK THEY USE IS ACTUALLY PRETTY RAD.

Striders were part of the fight to recover what was lost in the early days of the war. A Camera Strider is essentially a gun platform equipped with cameras. They were fairly effective against aerial attacks, though the Toilets targeted them from the air too (file 13). The Alliance largely withdrew them from the battlefield to work on an upgraded version.

SPEAKER STRIDER

These have only one attack, but it's an effective one—a sound wave blast (file 25). Anyone operating alongside a Speaker Strider should wear headphones to avoid damage.

The Toilets have copied the Alliance's Strider technology. The Alliance has to constantly develop new tech and get some kind of advantage from it before the Toilets get their own version!

THE NEW, IMPROVED CAMERA STRIDERS ARE NOW IN OPERATION (FILE 72), WITH HEAVIER WEAPONRY—FOUR PLASMA CANNONS INSTEAD OF ONE—AND GREATER POWER.

GLITCHMOBILE

The Alliance created this small flying craft by dismantling the Glitch Skibidi Toilet and adapting the toilet's bowl into a vehicle (file 63).

SPEED DEMON

It has the same glitch ability as the Glitch Toilet, so could move at high speed and ram opponents. It was also equipped with spikes to enhance those ram attacks, and plunger launchers mounted on each side.

Hell yeah. I didn't even ask for those. Scientist Cameraman just thought I'd like them. It's a lot cooler than the Toilet Car, I gotta say.

THE GLITCHMOBILE PLAYED AN IMPORTANT ROLE IN THE SIEGE OF ALPHA-HILLS, ENABLING PLUNGERMAN TO TAKE DOWN THE LASER STRIDER SKIBIDI TOILET (FILE 66). UNFORTUNATELY IT WAS WRECKED IN THE BATTLE WITH THE CHIEF SCIENTIST TOILET (FILE 67). I HAVE SUGGESTED WE MIGHT ADAPT THE GLITCH TECHNOLOGY TO CREATE A NEW VEHICLE, BUT THE GLITCHMOBILE IS SO FIRMLY ASSOCIATED WITH PLUNGERMAN, IT SEEMS LIKE NO ONE WANTS TO TAKE IT OVER FROM HIM.

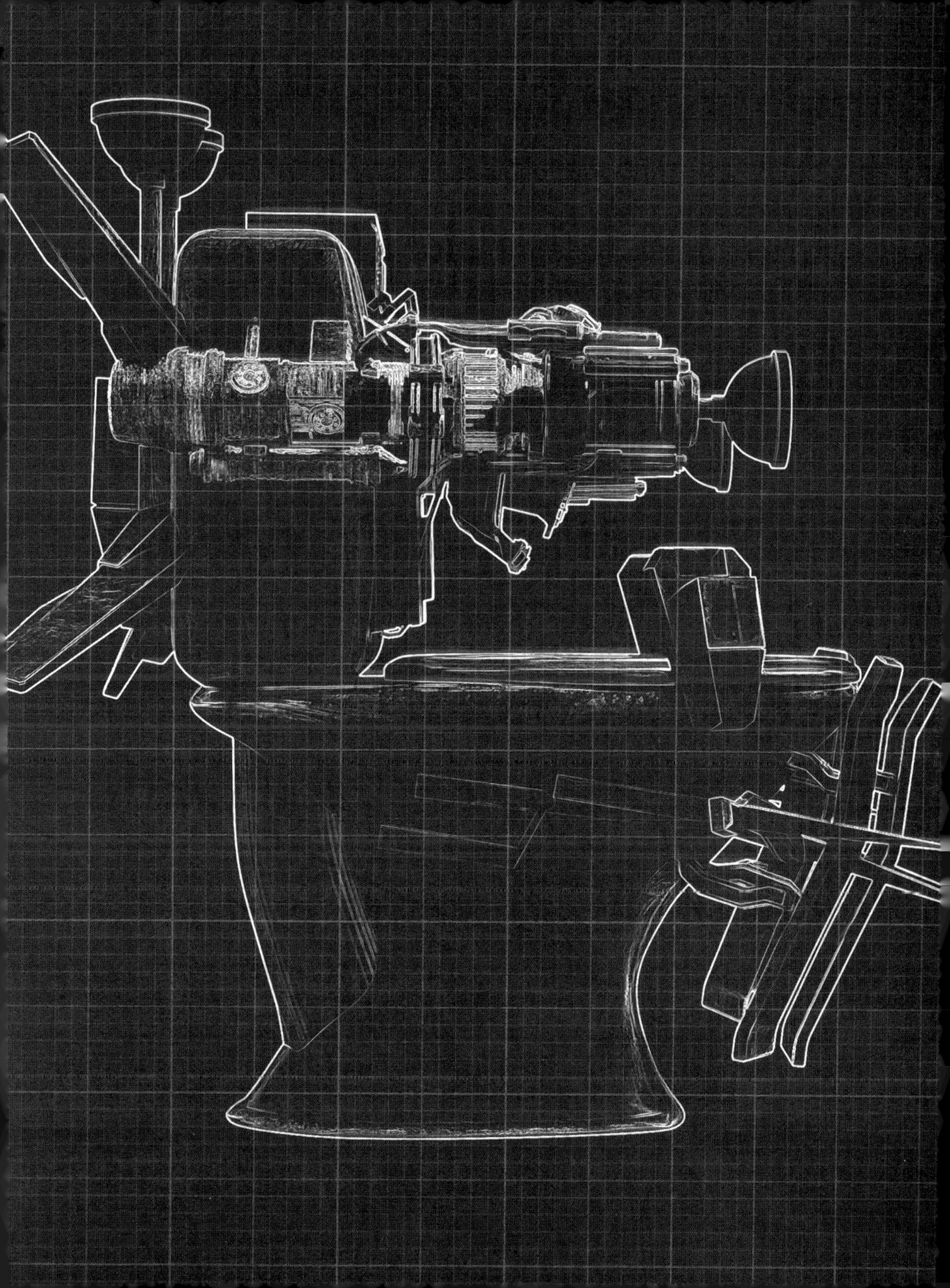

CAMERA HELICOPTER

In the early days of the war, the Alliance often used Camera Dropships to transport troops into and out of the battlefield (file 13). However, these have mostly been superseded by Camera Helicopters, which are more maneuverable (file 52). These have a cabin in the shape of a CCTV camera and are equipped with weaponry, but this is rarely used—their main purpose is to bring medical assistance, transport injured troops to safety so they can receive attention, or bring reinforcements.

I DID ASK OUR SCIENTISTS HOW THIS HELICOPTER FLIES WITHOUT A TAIL ROTOR TO STOP IT SPINNING AROUND RANDOMLY. APPARENTLY IT'S GOT GRAVITIC STABILIZERS FITTED TO EACH SIDE, WHICH REGULATE ITS MOVEMENT.

SPEAKER HELICOPTER

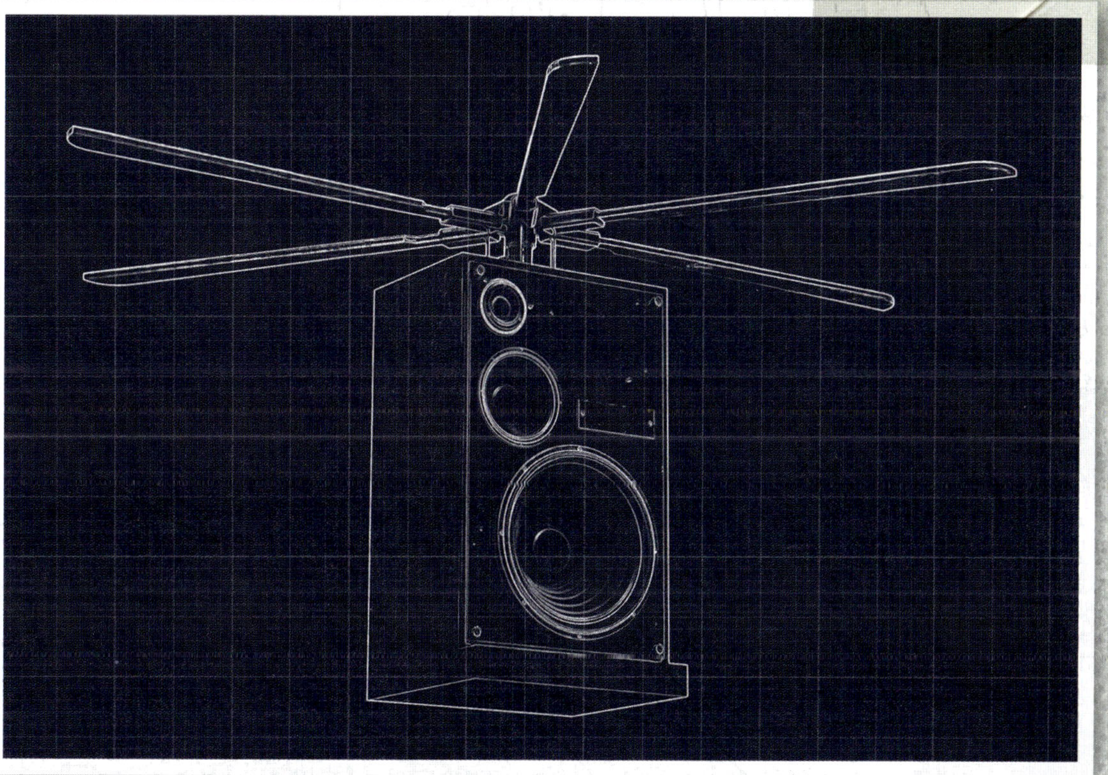

These have also been referred to as Stereocopters. Some observers assumed they were drones or vehicles, but they are, in fact, Speakerman variants who consist only of a 50-foot speaker body fitted with rotors (file 24). They can emit powerful sound waves that can knock opponents back, making them valuable support troops. Variant Speaker Helicopters have been used to make field repairs and upgrades—they've been seen carrying and fitting new plasma cannons to Titan Speakerman.

HEADPHONES

Headphones were originally developed by the Alliance as a protective device, not from Skibidi attacks but from the Alliance's own weapons. The sound waves emitted by the Strider Speaker could affect any Alliance fighters in the vicinity, making protection necessary (file 25). However, the Skibidi Toilets got wise to this and started using the headphones themselves to protect against such attacks (file 57).

WHILE CAMERAMEN, SPEAKERMEN, AND TV MEN DON'T NEED TO USE HEADPHONES TO PROTECT THEMSELVES FROM INFECTION BY THE SKIBIDI ANTHEM, THEY ARE EFFECTIVE PROTECTION FOR ANY SURVIVING HUMANS (FILES 73 AND 74).

SUNGLASSES

To the frustration of the Alliance, the Skibidi Toilets found a way of countering the TV Men's hypnosis attacks, creating sunglasses that filter out the red light. However, these sunglasses are breakable, so if they can be shattered during battle, it's still possible for a hypnosis attack to get through.

THE SKIBIDI TOILETS HAVE CONTINUED TO WORK ON THEIR SUNGLASSES TECHNOLOGY, INTRODUCING YELLOW GLASSES WORN BY G-TOILET (FILE 49). THEY'VE ALSO INTRODUCED GOGGLES, WHICH PERFORM THE SAME FUNCTION AS SUNGLASSES BUT ARE HARDER TO BREAK (FILE 46). GOGGLES CAN, HOWEVER, BE RIPPED OFF THE WEARER FAIRLY EASILY, SO IN A CLOSE COMBAT SITUATION, GO FOR THE GOGGLES.

JETPACKS

With many Skibidi Toilets possessing the power of flight, it was essential for the Alliance to develop their own equipment to enable them to engage in aerial combat. The first notable use of jetpack technology was in the battle between Titan Cameraman and G-Toilet (file 20), after which an increasing number of Toilets could also be seen using them.

Many different designs of jetpack have been used, including versions fitted with wings and ones that use a thruster to enhance horizontal movement.

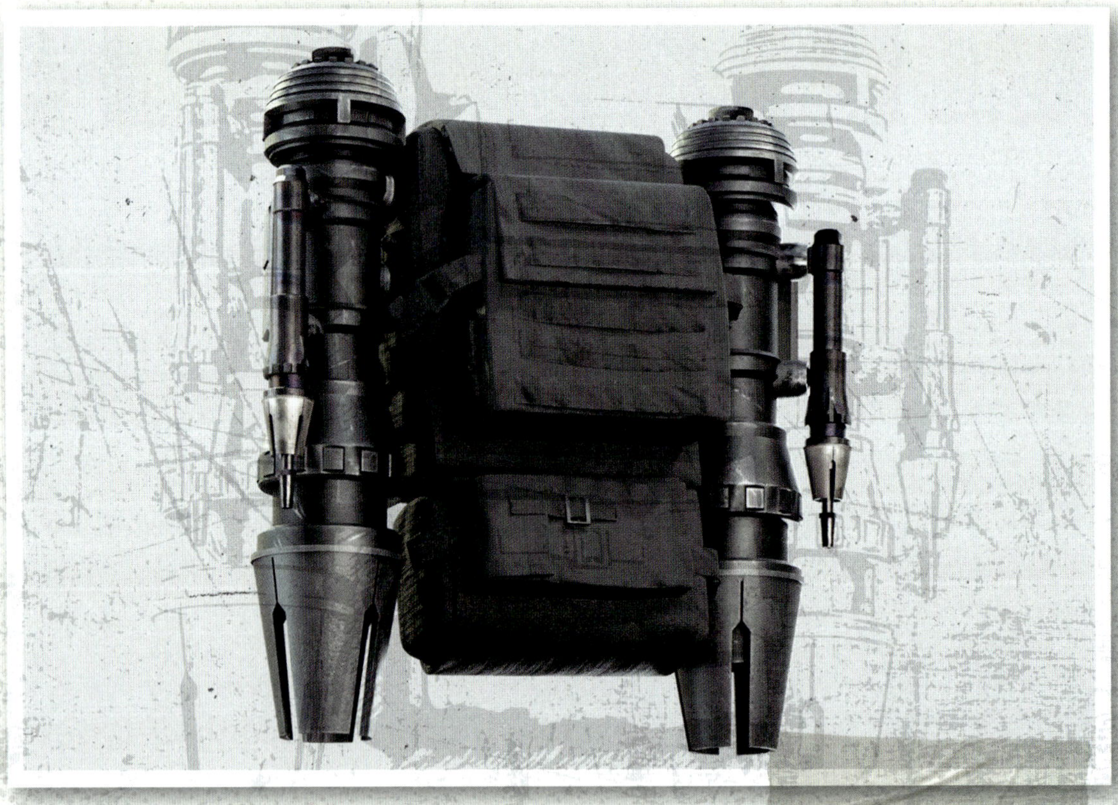

SHIELDS

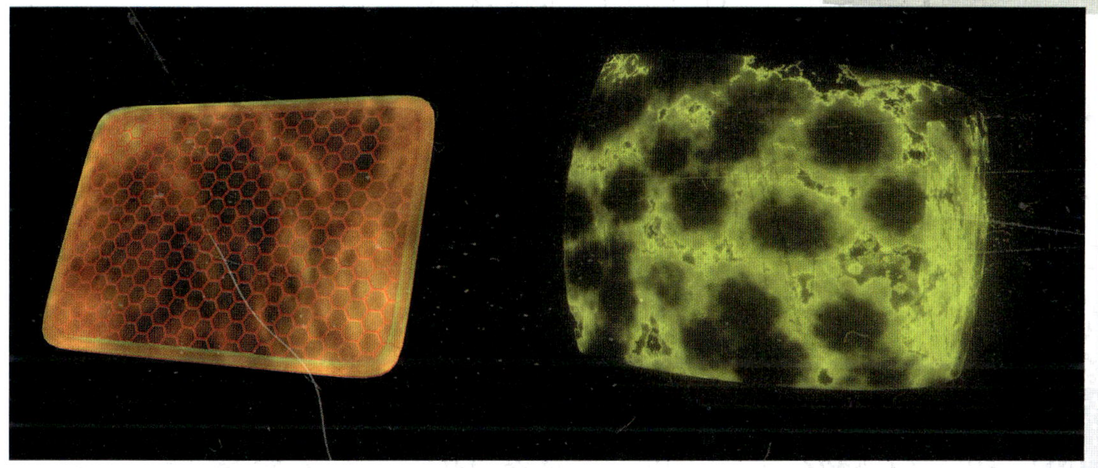

Combatants in the war have used physical shields and energy-based ones. Titan Cameraman has used a vast ballistic shield in combat, with a window that allows him to see while remaining covered (file 20).

The Alliance has subsequently developed energy-based shields that project a plasma barrier. These are highly effective at deflecting attacks of all kinds, and Titan Cameraman has been fitted with one (file 63). The Skibidi Toilets have created their own versions of these, and the Astro Toilets possess even stronger energy shields, which use a hexagonal formation (file 72).

Which is all good, but I wish he'd find somewhere to store it instead of leaving it leaning against buildings. If that thing falls over, it could crush somebody!

THE FUTURE

Where do we go from here? At one time it seemed possible we were dealing with an isolated attack from an enemy that had managed to replicate itself after arriving on Earth. If that was all it was, we could have destroyed them and moved on with our lives.

But now we know there's an Astro Toilet empire out there. And after a period where it seemed we were turning the tide of the war, now we're facing an even stronger enemy. But there is hope. We thought all the humans had been killed in the original invasion—but some survived, and there may be more.

We need to keep developing better tech and more powerful weapons—and we will. But we also need more information. Anything we learn may help us. Which is why I've preserved these notes—on paper, too, rather than a digital file that can easily get corrupted or wiped. If you find it, copy it, pass it on. The future will need to know these things.

I will make one prediction. If we ever get through this, I don't think anyone will ever find toilets funny again.

DAILY NEWS

BUSINESS • POLITICS • ECONOMICS • ENTERTAINMENT • SPORTS • WEATHER

BRAINROT CLAIMS "NONSENSE"

SAYS HEALTH SECRETARY

Growing public concern over reports that people are finding themselves unable to think or do anything except sing the same song over and over have been dismissed by the Health Secretary at the emergency conference last night.

"The brains of people in this country are fresher than they have ever been," he remarked. "Anyone complaining of difficulty thinking probably just needs to go on a detox, get back to nature."

When it was suggested to him that this was too complacent, he replied, "Skibidi dop dop dop yes yes, skibidi dabudu neep neep. We ain't here to hurt nobo